10

D0065130

The
CHOCOLATE
Pirate
Plot

The CHOCOLATE Pirate Plot

· A CHOCOHOLIC MYSTERY ·

JoAnna Carl

AN OBSIDIAN MYSTERY

OBSIDIAN
Published by New American Library,
a division of Penguin Group (USA) Inc.,
375 Hudson Street, New York, New York 10014, USA
Penguin Group (Canada), 90 Eglinton Avenue East, Suite 700, Toronto,
Ontario M4P 2Y3, Canada (a division of Pearson Penguin Canada Inc.)
Penguin Books Ltd., 80 Strand, London WC2R 0RL, England
Penguin Ireland, 25 St. Stephen's Green, Dublin 2,
Ireland (a division of Penguin Books Ltd.)
Penguin Group (Australia), 250 Camberwell Road, Camberwell,
Victoria 3124, Australia (a division of Pearson Australia Group Pty. Ltd.)
Penguin Books India Pvt. Ltd., 11 Community Centre,
Panchsheel Park, New Delhi - 110 017, India
Penguin Group (NZ), 67 Apollo Drive, Rosedale, North Shore 0632,
New Zealand (a division of Pearson New Zealand Ltd.)
Penguin Books (South Africa) (Pty.) Ltd., 24 Sturdee Avenue,
Rosebank, Johannesburg 2196, South Africa

Penguin Books Ltd., Registered Offices:
80 Strand, London WC2R 0RL, England

First published by Obsidian, an imprint of New American Library,
a division of Penguin Group (USA) Inc.

First Printing, October 2010
1   3   5   7   9   10   8   6   4   2

LIBRARY OF CONGRESS CATALOGING-IN-PUBLICATION DATA:
Carl, JoAnna.
The chocolate pirate plot: a chocoholic mystery/JoAnna Carl.
p.   cm.
ISBN 978-0-451-23127-7
1. McKinney, Lee (Fictitious character)—Fiction. 2. Women detectives—Fiction. 3. Chocolate
industry—Fiction. 4. Michigan—Fiction. I. Title.
PS3569.A51977C489   2010
813'.54—dc22   2010020127

Set in Stempel Garamond • Designed by Elke Sigal

Printed in the United States of America

Acknowledgments

Many thanks to Lake Michigan boating experts Tom Bolhuis and Judy and Phil Hallisy; law officers Jim Avance and Bob Swartz; Michigan neighbors Tracy Paquin and Susan McDermott; theater experts Scott and Peg Hoffmann; magician Marty Ludlum; all-around good guy Albert Anderson; music expert Jan Logan; and chocolatier Elizabeth Garber. They were all generous with information, and if I got it wrong, it's my fault, not theirs.

Chapter 1

A sunset cruise on Lake Michigan in an antique wooden powerboat is the perfect way to celebrate the summer solstice, and the weather that particular June 21 was also perfect.

Joe's Shepherd Sedan, a 1948 model he'd restored until it looked and ran like new, was anchored in a broad cove, so the boat was surrounded by a semicircle of sandy shore and tall trees. The four of us had finished our picnic dinner and were starting on coffee. With it we passed around bonbons and truffles made by TenHuis Chocolade—an easy contribution from me, since I work there as business manager.

We had clumped ourselves into a conversational group inside the boat's cabin—a cabin that was much like the interior of an automobile of the 1940s, except that where the trunk should have been there was a small deck.

The huge red sun had just sizzled and sunk into the water over toward Wisconsin. The breeze was cool, but not chilly; sweatshirts were nice, but inside the cabin jackets weren't needed. The water was a deep silky gray, the sky had exactly the right number of puffy purple clouds edged in gold, and gentle waves rocked the boat, making me feel as relaxed as a bird dozing off in its nest.

I was taking a bite of an Amaretto truffle as the pirate came over the stern.

His head popped up first. It was wrapped in a bandana, buccaneer style, and sported a big, bushy beard and a gold earring.

I was looking straight at the head as it appeared, but I was so surprised that all I did was blink.

Pirates on Lake Michigan? In the twenty-first century? Who could blame me if I didn't believe my eyes?

Then the pirate somersaulted over the side and leaped to his feet on the deck.

I leaped to my feet, too, banging my head on the sedan's roof. I probably yelled something witty, like, "Who the heck is that?"

The pirate wore black knee britches and a black vest, open to show a hairy, muscular chest. A pirate pistol was jammed into his broad belt, and he was brandishing a cutlass. Add that to the beard, bandana, and earring—plus a skull and crossbones tattoo on his biceps—and there was no question of what he represented.

The pirate waved his cutlass. He gave a loud yell, the traditional "Yo-ho-ho!"

My husband, Joe, and our friends Maggie and Ken McNutt were also on their feet as two more swimmers in pirate garb climbed over the stern.

The second pirate's outfit was almost identical to that of the first, except that over his bandana he had put on a funny hat with the brim flipped backward. He produced a whistle and began to play a rollicking sea chantey. Or I guess that's what it was.

The third pirate—a buccaneer queen whose vest had a plunging neckline that revealed her cleavage—began to dance, waving her arms in the air and weaving her feet into an intricate jig.

For the next two or three minutes the pirates went wild. The musician pranced, and the dancer danced. The first pirate waved his cutlass—by then I could see that it was plastic—in a series of fencing moves. He yelled in a hoarse voice, "Avast, me hearties!" and "Lift up the top sheet and spank her!" He clenched the cutlass in his teeth and did a handstand on the gunwale—the low railing along the side of the boat. Next he clembered onto the top of the cabin—we could hear his footsteps as he crossed over our heads—and dropped onto the bow. I peeked outside and saw that he was walking around on his hands, weaving among the horns, radio gear, and other paraphernalia the Coast Guard requires.

All this activity made the twenty-two-foot boat bob and buck. Joe, Ken, Maggie, and I each grabbed our coffee before it could spill. We held on to any parts of the boat we could reach as the dancing and acrobatics made it bounce around. The show was terrific—after our initial surprise we all started laughing—but I was afraid that the jumping around was going to knock one of the pirates overboard.

The buxom pirate queen didn't seem to share my fear. She linked arms with the piper, and then performed a do-si-do while he managed to continue playing.

Then the music stopped abruptly, and so did the dancing. The dancer and the musician gestured dramatically toward the front of the boat and the pirate who had boarded first.

"Yo-ho-ho!" His shout echoed over the water. He pulled the pistol from his belt and aimed it toward our group, right through the windshield.

I wasn't frightened. Despite their grotesque makeup and out-of-nowhere appearance, the pirates had done nothing but amaze and entertain us. I was wondering whether Ken or Joe had hired them as some sort of joke. Besides, the pistol was patently fake—an imitation firearm, a stage prop. I couldn't believe it would actually fire.

So the pointed pistol didn't make me faint. The pirate king simply couldn't be threatening us.

Then he pulled the trigger, and a flag popped out of the end of the gun. BANG! it said.

We all laughed hysterically. I guess we *were* hysterical.

Just as quickly as they had arrived, the pirates left. One by one they dived over the side of the boat, and Ken, Maggie, Joe, and I crowded out of the cabin and stood on the small open deck to look after them. All of us were laughing.

"Who were those masked men?" Ken said.

I hoisted my coffee cup. "Didn't you hire them, Ken?"

"Where would I find pirates to hire? Joe? Did you find a troupe of acrobatic pirates someplace?"

"Not me. Maggie? Are they from the Showboat Theater?"

"No!" Maggie, who teaches speech and drama at our local high school, was an actor and assistant director at our local repertory theater that summer. "At least I haven't heard anything about a pirate act."

Joe was leaning over the side. "Where did they go?" I realized that none of the swimming pirates had come up again.

"I never heard of mermaids—or mermen—in Lake Michigan," Maggie said. "And these pirates didn't have tails. So they must have a boat."

We scanned the horizon. Ken and I exclaimed at the same moment, "There it is!"

Sure enough, around a hundred feet away, just outside the cove, was an inflatable boat, the kind Navy SEALs use. None of us had noticed it earlier, and I still don't know how the pirates got that close without attracting our attention. As we watched, bandanas popped up on the gently rolling surface of the lake. The pirates continued to swim, now with their heads above the water's surface. Within minutes all of them reached their boat, and one by one the pirate crew climbed into it. They waved to us. Their outboard motor roared, and they left, throwing up spray behind them. The backwash reached our boat, bouncing us up and down. The pirate boat headed north, parallel to the shore, and was soon out of sight.

Ken, Maggie, Joe, and I stared after them.

"That was the oddest experience I've ever had on Lake Michigan," Joe said. "Or anyplace else."

Ours was the first boat boarded in what came to be known as the Summer of the Warner Pier Pirates.

Chapter 2

Maggie, Ken, Joe, and I all assumed that the pirates were some sort of promotional stunt. Warner Pier—Michigan's quaintest summer resort—was already full of pirates that year. We weren't too surprised that a few more had turned up.

The pirate craze was Marco Spear's fault. That was the year of his first big hit movie, *Young Blackbeard*. The film had everything: comedy, romance, a beautiful Caribbean setting, a cast of thousands, gorgeous costumes and sets—plus *action! action! action!* It also had a handsome and charismatic lead actor who did his own stunts.

America's teenagers gathered in gangs outside movie theaters and chanted his name. "Marco! Marco! Marco!"

My stepsister, Brenda McKinney, was working at Ten-Huis Chocolade again that summer, and she admitted that she'd seen *Young Blackbeard* twice. And she was nineteen and a sophomore in college, a little old for the fad. Marcia Herrera, the niece Joe and I had acquired when his mom remarried the previous spring, had just turned thirteen, so she was exactly the right age for the Marco craze. She had a half dozen Marco photos taped up inside her Warner Pier Middle

School locker, she told me, and she and her friends had each seen *Young Blackbeard* at least five times. She brought me a magazine showing pictures of Marco Spear from infancy to age twenty-two. It had ragged edges because of the number of times it had been read.

Some of the pictures showed Marco in his *Young Blackbeard* getup of tight knee britches and open vest with three days' stubble on his chin. Other pictures showed him in his pre–movie star life as an Olympic gymnastics champion. For those pictures he wore a tight, sleeveless shirt and those stirrup pants male gymnasts wear for competition. At thirty-one, I was too old for the Marco epidemic, but I was young enough to notice that he looked great in either outfit. Of course, the critics claimed he couldn't act nearly as well as he could swashbuckle, but America's girls didn't seem to care.

Marco Spear was clean-cut enough to please the mothers, athletic enough to impress the guys, and sexy enough to attract the girls. That and a major publicity campaign had put him at the pinnacle of celebrity. The guy couldn't move without falling over a member of the paparazzi. The world received daily updates on Marco's life, whether it wanted them or not.

Because of the topic of his first movie as the leading man, Marco had made pirates celebrities, too. The whole country was wearing eye patches and growling, "Arrr."

Naturally, Warner Pier had gotten on board for the fad. Our chamber of commerce had picked "Warner Pier: A Lake Michigan Treasure" as the slogan for the summer and had selected a logo featuring a buccaneer waving a cutlass and hoisting a treasure chest on his shoulder. Teenagers costumed as pirates roamed our picturesque downtown, handing out golden coins and treasure maps to tourists. A weekly Treasure

Hunt sale offered special bargains to shoppers. The climactic production of our summer repertory theater was to be *The Pirates of Penzance*, with Maggie McNutt in the role of Ruth, the pirates' maid.

Even my aunt, Nettie TenHuis Jones, president and chief chocolatier of TenHuis Chocolade, was involved. Our featured items for the summer were pirate treasure chests—four-inch, six-inch, and eight-inch—filled with chocolate coins and jewels covered with shiny gold or silver foil. A giant pirate ship made of chocolate was the centerpiece of our show window. The Jolly Roger that flew from its mast was made of dark chocolate, with the skull and crossbones painted on the banner with white chocolate. The sails were white chocolate, and the decks milk chocolate. It was a work of art—but just for looking, not for eating. Aunt Nettie would kill anybody if they took a bite.

Pirates were everywhere in Warner Pier. So when Joe's meticulously restored wooden boat was boarded by pirates in Lake Michigan—and those pirates did nothing but entertain us—we thought it was yet another commercial promotion.

I'm half Texan, half Michigan Dutch. I had always lived in Texas until I came to Warner Pier three years ago. I came because I needed a new start after ditching my first husband, the one I should never have married to begin with, and because my aunt needed a business manager for her chocolate company.

Warner Pier was my mother's hometown. I'd worked for Aunt Nettie when I was a teenager, so I wasn't a complete stranger, and in the past three years I'd grown to love the place. I also grew to love the chocolate business. And I fell madly in love with a guy named Joe Woodyard.

Joe is a Warner Pier native who first gained local fame at seventeen, when he won top state honors in high school wrestling and high school debate the same year. When I first saw Joe, he was in college and working as a lifeguard at Warner Pier Beach, and I was one of the girls who stood around on the sand admiring his shoulders. We moved in different circles then, and our circles didn't overlap until ten years later.

Joe graduated from the University of Michigan, went to law school, practiced poverty law, and—like me—made a really dumb first marriage, to a nationally known defense attorney. When the marriage ended, he was so disgusted that he quit practicing law. He opted to become "an honest craftsman," or so he told me when we got acquainted. He bought a small business, Vintage Boats, and began restoring antique powerboats.

I admire Joe's brains, character, and abilities, but I'll admit I was initially attracted to him because I think he's the best-looking guy in west Michigan. Black hair, bright blue eyes, and terrific shoulders. Mmm, mmm. Besides, he's six feet two, and since I'm just a shade under six feet myself—well, it's nice to be with a guy I don't look down on.

By the time the pirates boarded our boat on the evening of the summer solstice, we'd been married for fifteen months and Joe was edging back into practicing law. He had first held a one-day-a-week job as Warner Pier's city attorney. Then, when his mother married the mayor—it's a long story—he quit his city job to avoid any appearance of nepotism, and he joined a legal aid–type organization in Holland, thirty miles north of us. That summer he was commuting up there two or three days a week.

But Joe loves those antique powerboats. To Joe, our picnic

on the water in the 1948 Shepherd with Maggie and Ken had been an ideal evening.

Maggie and Ken are what used to be called "a teaching couple." Both are on the faculty of Warner Pier High School, and both are good at what they do. Ken's math students bring home all sorts of honors, and Maggie's pupils routinely win state speech and drama awards. The kids are terribly impressed by Maggie—she "worked in Hollywood," they whisper. And it's true that Maggie made a few movies, but if anyone brings up that part of her life, she changes the subject.

Like Joe and me, Ken and Maggie are in their early thirties. Maggie's tiny and vivacious, with dark hair, and Ken is lanky and thin, with limp and colorless hair. They both have extremely sharp brains.

All four of us thought our solstice adventure had been an amusing experience, and we told everybody about the pirates.

Joe passed the story along to a group he meets for coffee most mornings at the Shell station out on the highway. Its regulars include a carpenter, a furniture maker, a home builder, and a roofing contractor, so I call it "the Craft Klatch." Ken told the story to the faculty at the math and computer camp where he was teaching that summer. I told everybody at the chocolate shop, and Maggie spread the word around the theater. So by noon, news of our experience was all over town, and I got a call from Chuck O'Riley, editor of our local weekly newspaper, the *Warner Pier Gazette*.

I assured Chuck that we hadn't been injured or even inconvenienced, just amused.

"We all assumed it was some sort of promotional stunt," I said. "But the pirates didn't give us any information."

"Maybe it's *The Pirates of Penzance*," Chuck said.

"Could be."

But after lunch, Max Morgan, the director of the Warner Pier Summer Showboat, came into the shop. He has a picture of himself as Falstaff in his office at the theater, but he'd required a lot of padding to play that part. Max is short and scrawny, with a dark fringe of hair surrounding a bald spot. Max ignored the counter girls on duty and came straight to my office. "Lee!" He has the resonant voice that comes from dramatic training, and he used his standard booming tones. "Where can I find these pirates of yours?"

"They're not my pirates," I said. "We thought they might be yours. Did you hire them to publicize *The Pirates of Penzance*?"

"No! But it's a great promotional idea. I want to get hold of them."

"It shouldn't be too hard. Just check at Warner Pier Beach."

"Why there?"

"Because athletes like those will be showing off their muscles someplace."

"They had muscles, huh?"

"They were genuine acrobats. They somersaulted over the side of the boat. One of them walked on his hands on the gunwale. The girl pirate did a sailor's hornpipe, or a jig of some sort. One played the pennywhistle. Then they dived overboard, swam underwater for a long way, and seemed to vault into their boat. And that water was cold, but it didn't seem to bother them. They gave an impressive show."

"What did they look like?"

"They looked like fake beards and overdone eye makeup, Max. I couldn't tell anything about their faces."

"Try."

"There was a woman, a well-endowed woman, and two men. One of the men was larger and hairier than the other one was. But all three of them wore heavy makeup. I wouldn't know them if they were—" I gestured at four tourists who were staring at the pirate ship in our window. "Without the makeup and costumes, I wouldn't know them if they were standing outside that window."

Max continued to quiz me. He seemed quite eager to hire the three pirates to help promote the Gilbert and Sullivan production planned for August. The more I told him that I couldn't tell him anything definite, the harder he pressed.

Finally I'd had enough. "Max! Ask around the beach. Ask at the summer camps."

Max looked startled. "Summer camps? Why do you suggest summer camps?"

"Because that's where student athletes and coaches get summer jobs. Or you could try the health club."

Max took that suggestion more calmly. "The health club?"

"Sure. The one out by the highway. That's where you'll find those athletic types. But I haven't got time to go looking for them."

Max smiled slyly.

I gestured at the chocolate counter. "This is TenHuis Chocolade, Max. Everybody gets a free sample. Pick a bonbon or a truffle and go away."

Max selected a Jamaican rum truffle ("the ultimate dark chocolate truffle"). He went away, but he said he wasn't happy. He still wanted to find the pirates.

Later I learned that Max also cornered Joe, Ken, and Maggie to give each of them the third degree. But none of them could identify the pirates either.

Max even ran an ad—a whole quarter page—in the *Gazette*, offering employment to the pirates who had boarded us. But no one replied.

By the next weekend, the excitement had died down. I yawned and concentrated on running a chocolate company.

Then, the next Monday, the pirates struck again.

Once more they appeared just at sunset, climbing aboard a small yacht that was taking a group on an evening cruise. Again they gave an exciting demonstration of acrobatics. This time all three walked on their hands—the girl even did an aerial cartwheel, that spectacular flip in which the hands don't touch the ground. The piper did a few sleight-of-hand tricks.

Again the people on the boat applauded and cheered as the three dived into the water and swam underwater a long way, then climbed into their inflatable dinghy and roared away, leaving the boaters with a darn good story.

Max Morgan went absolutely crazy. He came to see Joe at home. "I must find those guys," he said.

"I can't help you."

"Joe, can't you identify their boat?"

"I don't see how, Max. It's an inflatable dinghy. You know, a plastic shell for a bottom with sides like big, tough balloons. There's one trailing behind every cabin cruiser and every yacht docked at every Warner Pier marina."

"But you know boats, Joe! Surely you can tell more than that."

"Not in the dusk, Max. Not at that distance. It was too far away for me to tell if the dinghy had a patch or a name stenciled on the side. It's larger than the usual dinghy, but that's not a lot of help."

Max turned to me. "Lee, what about their costumes?"

I considered. "I'd guess that they were made from old wet suits."

"Wet suits?"

"Yes. I think they cut the legs and arms off wet suits. I'm sure the girl's sexy outfit zips down the front like a wet suit. As for the wigs and makeup—you've got people at the theater who know more about that than I do. Ask them."

Max growled. "They've got ideas about how the makeup could be done, but they haven't seen them in person."

He left, huffy.

But the pirates didn't leave. Eight times they struck in July. Always early in the week and occasionally on Sunday evenings. Warner Pier's boaters began to brag about being hit by the pirates. It became a point of pride. People gave "pirate parties" and were disappointed if they weren't boarded.

After sundown, boats would slide into their slips at the marinas with decks full of passengers, all yelling and laughing hilariously and bragging. "We were boarded!"

Max finally gave up trying to identify and hire the pirates.

I lost all curiosity about them early. Running a chocolate business and trying to find some time to spend with Joe took all my energy. I had no interest in fake pirates who could walk on their hands. The evening we were boarded faded into memory. The *Gazette* still ran stories, but Chuck O'Riley had moved them to an inside page.

I was glad to see interest in the pirates wane, but I wasn't ready for a new kind of excitement.

That began on the last Wednesday in July.

My office is a glass-walled cubical at one side of the Ten-Huis Chocolade retail store. There was only one customer in the store, and I was working quietly in my office when the street door flew open with such violence that I expected the window in it to shatter.

Two of our counter girls ran in—my stepsister, Brenda, and her best pal, Tracy Roderick. They were traveling at hurricane speed and shrieking like hurricane winds.

I jumped up. "What's wrong? Why all the yelling?"

"Marco's coming! Marco's coming!"

"What?"

"Marco Spear is coming to Warner Pier!"

Chapter 3

This behavior was most unlike Tracy and Brenda. Both were ready for their second year of college. Being cool was a full-time job for them, and despite a running argument between Brenda and her boyfriend over Marco Spear's acting ability, movie-star crushes were not their idea of cool.

But Tracy's next squeal showed me I was wrong. "It's so great! To think, we might get to see him!"

They jumped up and down and squealed some more. The two girls already at work behind the counter came out and joined in the squealing and jumping. The lone customer, who was a nerdy-looking young man, shrank back against the front door.

The girls' enthusiasm got a bit out of hand. As they jumped around in their excitement, Tracy got too close to the big, beautiful pirate ship in the window.

"Look out!" Brenda tried to warn her, but Tracy didn't hear. She kept backing toward the window—and the ship. She was shaking her fists above her head. She had no idea she was about to hit the ship. I'm sure my face was full of horror. Brenda's was, too, and even the nerdy customer was yelling, "Stop!"

That ship—representing hundreds of dollars worth of

chocolate and a week of skilled work—was about to hit the floor.

But a miracle happened. The nerdy customer leaped through the group of whirling girls. He slid in next to the table that held the ship. And he grabbed it. Gently.

The ship teetered. The Jolly Roger appeared actually to wave. But the ship stayed upright.

At last all four of the excited girls saw what had nearly happened. They froze. There was a mass intake of breath. Then everyone exhaled in unison, and absolute silence fell.

"Thank you," I said to the customer. "We are eternally in your debt."

The young man smiled. "Glad I could be of help."

For the first time, I looked at him as a person rather than as an anonymous customer. He had buckteeth and wore thick glasses, the kind that distort the wearer's face. He seemed to be in his early twenties, but his plaid shorts weren't exactly what the Warner Pier college crowd was wearing. His sneakers were the wrong brand, and he wore a floppy sports shirt rather than the T-shirt required by Warner Pier fashion.

I addressed the four girls. "Now, shall we get back to business? First, someone give this young man a pound of chocolates. He's saved the day. Or the ship."

Looking shamefaced—as they should have—the four girls scurried. The two on duty went back to their stations near the cash register. Tracy and Brenda took the customer through our flavors of truffles and bonbons, helping him to select the thirty-two it took to fill a one-pound box.

The young man seemed embarrassed. He assured us that he needed no reward, but I insisted. "Give them to your mother," I said. Somehow I doubted this guy had a girlfriend.

I was happy to see that Brenda made an effort to talk to him, asking him whether he lived in Warner Pier permanently. He was from New Jersey, he told her, and was here for a few weeks. That put him firmly in the "tourist" category.

Warner Pier has three social classes—locals, summer people, and tourists. Locals live here full-time, summer people rent or own property and stay all summer, and tourists stay for shorter times. It's a rigid caste system.

As soon as he'd left, I summoned Tracy and Brenda into my office. "What were y'all so excited about?" I tried to sound stern. "You two don't usually go nuts over movie stars."

"But Marco Spear is coming to Warner Pier!"

"Where did you hear this?"

"We stopped by the Superette, and Mr. Gossip—I mean, Mr. Glossop—told us that fancy new yacht Oxford Boats is building is for Marco Spear! And Marco's coming to Warner Pier—himself—in person—to pick it up!"

They barely restrained themselves from another squealing session.

"Tracy," I said, "how reliable do you find information provided by Greg Glossop?" Greg Glossop, who runs the pharmacy at our local supermarket, is well-known as the worst gossip in Warner Pier.

My question brought giggles from Brenda, and Tracy smiled sheepishly. "Oh, I know—he leaps to conclusions."

"He vaults to conclusions the way Marco Spear jumps up and down the masts of pirate ships."

"But there really is a gorgeous yacht out there—in the big building at Oxford Boats. Brenda and I saw it when we went out on the river with Will and Carl last week."

"Yes, Joe and I saw it, too, and I think it would be great if

Marco Spear bought it. But if Greg Glossop is spreading the story, I wouldn't hold my breath." I paused for effect. "Are you and Brenda reporting for work?"

After I thought it over, I wasn't unhappy for Brenda and Tracy to have some distraction from Will and Carl. Or at least it might be a good thing for Brenda. She wasn't my responsibility—I'd made sure my stepmother understood that before Brenda came to Michigan—but I was fond of her, and I didn't like the idea of her heart being broken. Or of her breaking Will's heart. They hadn't had a peaceful summer.

Brenda's mom married my dad when I was sixteen and Brenda was five. I lived with my mom, so I was part of the household only a few times a year. Because of this, Brenda and I had been practically strangers until the previous year, when Brenda came to Warner Pier for our wedding and met a big blond guy named Will VanKlompen. He'd made a strong enough impression that she asked me if she could come back and work for TenHuis Chocolade that summer.

Brenda's appearance is different from that of most Michigan girls, who, like me, tend to be built on the northern European pattern—tall and blond. I could see why Brenda's dark hair and eyes and cute rounded figure appealed to Will. And I could certainly see why a six-foot-two blond hunk like Will appealed to Brenda.

Their romance had gone fairly smoothly the previous summer. Conflicting work schedules had kept them from seeing each other every waking moment. They seemed to have fun without getting too involved emotionally. In August Brenda and Will had gone to their respective colleges with relatively few parting tears.

In the spring Will had urged Brenda to return to Warner

Pier for a second summer. Then Tracy's parents planned a two-month trip in their travel trailer, and they told Tracy she could stay in the family home if she found a friend to stay with her. They approved of Brenda for this role.

So everything seemed fine when Brenda arrived the first week in June, planning to visit Joe and me for a few days, then move to Tracy's house.

But on the second night she was there, things went to pieces.

Brenda had gone out with Will. Joe and I had decided to make it plain to her that we were not sitting up to check on when—or whether—she got home. Privately, the two of us had agreed that we'd retire to our own room before the eleven o'clock news.

But it wasn't even ten o'clock when car lights bounced down our lane and passed the house.

"That can't be Brenda already," Joe said.

"I wasn't expecting anyone else."

The car had barely had time to pull into our drive when a door slammed and we heard some indistinct words from Brenda. She ran in the back door and stopped in the kitchen. Then we could see the lights of Will's car moving again; he was pulling out of the drive.

I called out. "Brenda?"

She stayed where she was. I could hear gulping noises.

I went into the kitchen. "Brenda? Are you all right?"

"Yes." The word was affirmative, but the tone was negative.

"What's wrong?"

"Nothing! Nothing's wrong." She gave a huge sob, then ran up the stairs. "I'm going to bed!"

Joe and I watched her go. We looked at each other. "Well," I said, "I guess I won't ask if she had a good time."

"You should go up and talk to her."

"Sorry. If she wants to confide in me, she will. I'm not going to demand an explanation."

"But—"

"No, Joe. She'll explain when she wants to."

We resumed our seats in the living room. I had been reading, and Joe had been looking over some papers dealing with one of his cases. We continued to do this. But neither of us turned another page after Brenda came in.

Our old house is like an amplifier for any sound made in it. A pin dropped in one of the upstairs bedrooms sounds like an anvil landing on the ceiling of the living room. And Brenda was definitely louder than a pin. She would sob. Then she would sniff. Then she would mutter. She would walk up and down, stomping her feet. The sounds were unnerving.

After twenty minutes, Joe got to his feet. "I'm going to get in the truck and go track Will down," he said. "That guy needs a good talking to."

"Joe!"

"I mean it. I don't know what he did, but he had no right to make Brenda so miserable."

"No!" I jumped up. "Stay away from Will! I'll talk to Brenda."

The steep stairs that lead to the second floor of our house seemed to have grown even steeper as I went up them. If I tried to talk to her, how would Brenda react? Would there be tears? Yelling? Would she order me out of her room? Shove me back down the stairs? What should I say to her?

The door to her room was closed. I decided that knocking

was unwise, since she could just tell me I couldn't come in. I opened the door a crack and spoke.

"It's Lee. Ready to talk?"

I didn't wait for an answer. I just slipped inside.

Brenda was sitting on the opposite side of the bed, leaning back against two pillows. She was still dressed in jeans and a sweatshirt, though she'd kicked her tennis shoes off. Sodden tissues were heaped on the bed beside her. She didn't speak, or even look at me.

I sat down on the foot of the bed. "Do you think Joe can beat Will up?"

Brenda gasped. "Oh! Will's really strong! And Will's a lot—well, younger than Joe is."

"Yes, but Joe's wily. He was a wrestling champion, you know. And he's extremely mad at Will."

"Why?"

"Because Will made you unhappy."

She sobbed. "Why should Joe care?"

"You're our babysitter. I mean, sister!"

Brenda gave a funny little laugh, more like a hiccup. "Oh, Lee! You're so funny!"

"Lie down," I said. "I'll rub your back the way my grandmother used to rub mine."

I was rather surprised when Brenda complied, flopping onto her stomach. I stood up, leaned over her, and began to rub her shoulders. I didn't ask any questions, and she continued to cry quietly, but after about five minutes she spoke.

"Oh, Lee, it was awful! Will says Marco Spear can't act!"

Marco Spear couldn't act? That was what all this drama was about?

Somehow I managed to refrain from either laughing or

blurting out, "Whoever thought he could?" I just kept rubbing Brenda's back, and after I had control of myself I said, "How did this quarrel come up, Brenda?"

One of the activities Will and Brenda both enjoyed, of course, was movies. "I mean films," she said. So both had taken a college course in film criticism. "You know," Brenda said, "arts and humanities requirement."

Since *Young Blackbeard* had been the most popular film of the spring semester, each class—the one at Michigan State and the one at North Texas Junior College—had discussed it. Brenda had come away convinced that the film was a masterpiece and that Marco Spear's performance was worthy of an Academy Award. Will had been convinced that the movie was a piece of trash and that Marco Spear was a complete ham.

"It's not just that we disagree," Brenda said, sniffing.

"It's that he didn't respect your opinion," I said.

"No! He didn't! And besides"—she sobbed—"he said I only liked Marco Spear because he's s-s-sexy!"

I longed to laugh, but Brenda's emotional upset was too serious to take lightly. "Do you think Will could be jealous?"

"Of Marco Spear? That's silly! He's not a real person."

Of course, Marco Spear definitely was a real person, but I understood what Brenda meant.

At least the commotion gave Brenda and me a good reason to have a heart-to-heart talk, and I found out some interesting information.

Brenda wasn't at all sure how she felt about Will. He was "really, really nice." And a lot of fun. And she *liked* him. (I interpreted that as meaning she found him sexually attractive.) Yes, someday she might want to marry him. But back in Texas she was involved in activities and fun at the area junior college.

And there was another guy. "We've gone out since junior high. It's not *serious*!" (Did that mean she wasn't sexually attracted to him? Maybe. At least they weren't having sex.)

Plus, Brenda said, she had made plans to go on to Midwestern University in Wichita Falls for her junior and senior years. She wanted a degree in some sort of computer design.

I felt a great gush of relief at realizing that Brenda's ambitions were broader than getting married at nineteen and pregnant at twenty.

Brenda and I talked for quite a while. Then we went downstairs. She gave Joe a hug, and he gave her one back. "You don't have to whip Will," she said.

"I'm not sure I could."

"Thanks for wanting to. That's just what my daddy would do."

Joe gave me a quick look to make sure that remark was okay. He knows that I had trouble learning to share my daddy with another girl, even one much younger than I am. I couldn't do it until I figured out that Brenda's birth father had never been part of her life. My dad was all the daddy she had ever had.

Joe and I promised not to talk about Brenda and Will's fight to anybody. After we were in bed that night, we shared a giggle over the topic of the fight—talk about ridiculous—but we both understood that the fight hadn't really been about Marco Spear's acting ability. It had been about Brenda and Will learning to be honest with each other and to respect each other's opinions. Remembering that made it easier for me to take it seriously.

After that dramatic beginning, I was afraid Brenda's summer would be a disaster. She might even decide to go home. But she didn't feel she could leave Tracy. In a few days, she and

Will began to see each other again. Usually they went out with Tracy and her boyfriend, Carl, and they seemed to treat each other with caution, as if saying the wrong thing could cause an explosion.

The argument over Marco Spear's acting ability still erupted now and then, but mainly Brenda and Will ignored the subject. However, I suspected that part of Brenda's excitement over the possibility of Marco Spear's coming to Warner Pier was the fact that she could tease Will over it.

Whatever I thought, the rumor that he was coming spread through town. Marco! Marco! Marco!

The news was whispered down the aisles at the Superette and spoken out loud at Warner Pier Beach. Everybody was sure he was coming, although there was no official confirmation.

Warner Pier is the home of Oxford Boats, one of the last companies that build luxury yachts. Their products were not the boats you might see at a boat show or use for a fishing trip. Each yacht produced by Oxford Boats was individually designed by the nation's top maritime architect. The yachts took a year or more to build. Most of them carried from six to a dozen crew members when they left port. Their sleek hulls and luxurious cabins inspired as much drooling as TenHuis chocolates.

Oxford Boats' prices were in the multimillions. Someone once said that if you wonder how much it costs to own a yacht, you can't afford it anyway. Apparently Marco Spear had made enough money from *Young Blackbeard* that he didn't have to ask.

Every teenager who had access to a sailboat, motorboat, or dinghy was out on the water, peering into the big boat shed at Oxford Boats, trying to get a look at the yacht under construction.

Marco! Marco! Marco! He must be coming soon.

I got extremely tired of the whole thing. In fact, I tried to put it out of my mind completely. I wasn't worried about movie stars. I had plenty to think about in my own life.

Joe and I live in a semirural neighborhood on the inland side of Lake Shore Drive, and at about eight o'clock in the morning on the second Saturday in August I put on a pair of denim shorts, a sweatshirt, and some sandals and walked down to the road to get the *Grand Rapids Press* out of our delivery box. It was a bright, crisp morning. The sunlight was filtering through the trees, and the birds were singing like mad. I scared a flock of eight wild turkeys—two hens and six half-grown poults—out of our side yard as I left the house. It was my day off. I didn't have to rush down to the shop. All was serene.

I had barely reached the newspaper delivery box when the screaming started.

"Help! Help!"

I nearly dropped my newspaper as I whirled toward the sound. A girl wearing a neon-striped bikini came running up Lake Shore Drive toward me, a pair of orange flip-flops flip-flopping on her feet.

"He didn't come up! He just disappeared!"

As soon as she was within clutching distance, she grabbed my arm. Her fingers felt like so many vises. I could see that tears were running down her face.

"I'm afraid he's dead!"

"Who?"

"Jeremy! He said he was going to show me how to do a surface dive. But he never came up! I think he drowned."

Chapter 4

Two hours later I was sitting in my folding beach chair on the sand of Beech Tree Public Access Area, a quarter mile from our house. The temperature had just hit seventy-two degrees, and puffy white clouds floated here and there in the broad blue sky. August is one of the reasons Lake Michigan is a major resort area, and that day was a perfect demonstration of its perfect weather.

At the top of the bank behind me, delightful breezes wafted through twenty-five or so elms and maples and one giant beech tree, the tree that gave the beach its name. The sun had just climbed higher than the trees, so it was now beginning to reach the beach. I had brought a big multicolored umbrella; soon we'd need it for protection from the sun.

The idyllic setting contrasted with the activities on the beach. A half dozen people in law enforcement outfits—Warner Pier Police Department and Warner County Sheriff's Department—were talking on radios or standing in concerned clumps, staring out into the lake. There more than twenty people walked slowly through the water with their arms linked.

These were volunteers, mostly from our neighborhood,

and they were using their feet to search for the body of the missing swimmer. They formed a line anchored at the beach and walked through the water in a fan-shaped pattern, re-forming at the end of each sweep to cover a new area.

Although I had phoned in the first alarm, I was a minor part of the search. My job was keeping an eye on two things: first, a large cooler of bottled water for the volunteers in the lake; second, the missing man's girlfriend, the girl in the bright bikini. She was sitting beside me in a second beach chair.

Her name was Jill Campbell. I was assigned to keep any news media representatives away from her, unless she wanted to talk to them, and to make sure she didn't disappear, in case the rescuers needed to talk to her. Spectators were confined to the top of the bank behind us by yellow "do not cross" tape, of course, and the umbrella was supposed to shield her from the gaze of the merely curious as well as from the sun.

Jill seemed to be barely smart enough to fasten her bikini top. She had a sweetly pretty face, blond hair that was art-fully dark at the roots, and a figure a little too slim to properly display the neon-striped swimsuit that peeked out from her white terry-cloth beach wrap. Actually, it was *my* terry-cloth beach wrap. I'd loaned it to her. I was still wearing the shorts I'd put on to go get the newspaper, but I'd replaced my sweat-shirt with a tee, and I'd put on my own flip-flops.

Joe was one of the guys out in the lake, looking for Jeremy, the missing swimmer. Since he was among the tallest, he was also farthest out.

This wasn't my favorite way to spend a Saturday, the one day a week I don't have to work during the height of the sum-mer tourist season, but someone needed to sit with Jill.

Lake Michigan is an inland sea, 118 miles across at the

widest point between Michigan and Wisconsin, more than 300 miles long from the Indiana dunes to Mackinac Bridge, and 923 feet deep at its deepest spot. And it can have waves. Big waves. Luckily, that day they were only a couple of feet high, but since they were coming from the southwest, the water was cloudy.

If our summer visitors hang around beaches on the east side of Lake Michigan very long, they learn that if the wind is coming from the southwest, the water is, too. That water is warm—compared to ice water—but it's filled with sediment and waterweeds. At least we hope that's what makes it murky. It's coming straight from Chicago.

If the wind and water are coming from the northwest, the lake is clear but cold. If the wind is from the east, the beach is invaded by flies, and I don't want to go down there, so I have no idea what the water is like.

Looking for a body in Lake Michigan is not a one-man job. After Jill came to our house looking for help, I called 9-1-1, then contacted a few neighbors I knew were swimmers. They called other people. Joe put on his swim trunks and headed for the beach, taking Jill with him. Joe immediately made some dives in the area where Jill said her friend had gone down, but he hadn't found the missing Jeremy, and neither had other people who arrived on the scene within the next hour. Now the volunteers were doing their gruesome line dance, hoping one of them would stub a toe on Jeremy's body. If this didn't work, they'd go home, and in a couple of days helicopters would start patrolling the shoreline, looking for a body floating in the water or washed up on the beach.

By now Jill wasn't tearful. That was all right with me. Jill seemed familiar, which meant I'd probably seen her around town, but I didn't know her, and I didn't feel equipped to console a stranger's grief.

She hadn't wanted to talk a lot, which was surprising. My experience has been that people who've gone through traumatic experiences are eager to talk about them. But Warner Pier's police chief, Hogan Jones—who just happens to be married to my aunt—had trouble getting the whole story out of her.

Jeremy Mattox was the full name of the missing man, Jill had told him. She said he wasn't a serious boyfriend, just a casual date.

"He works where I work, and he offered to show me this beach. He said it was real nice, and they don't charge to use it. So he picked me up at seven, and we came up here."

I was curious, so I interrupted. "Why did you come so early?"

"Early?" Jill looked at me blankly.

"Yes." I tried to look encouraging. "Beaches in our part of Michigan face west. This one has a high bank behind it, and a lot of trees on top of the bank. There's never any sun here until late in the morning. Hardly anybody comes here to swim before noon."

"Oh. Well." She seemed to need a moment to think the question over. "We have to work this afternoon."

"Wasn't the beach cold when you got here?"

"Yes, but I brought a cover-up."

Jill's cover-up was a gauzy shirt that matched her neon-striped bikini. It was designed to keep the sun off, not keep the wearer warm when the temperature was around fifty-five in the shade, as it would have been before eight a.m. at Beech Tree Public Access Area.

She didn't have a lot more to say to Hogan or to me.

West Michigan was settled nearly two hundred years ago by the Dutch. Many of their descendants, including me, are still here, so lots of us look as if we just stepped out of the Zuider Zee. There are more people in the phone book named VanSomething-or-other than there are named Smith, and Dykstra is considered a common name.

So West Michigan is full of big, blond people. As a tall natural blond, I'd stood out in Texas. In west Michigan I rarely got a second glance.

Jill did not look like a west Michigan native. She was small, maybe five foot three, and—like Brenda—she seemed more exotic than the wholesome-looking Dutch girls of Warner Pier. She had dark eyes and a beautiful tan. Her hair was blond, true, but it was the frankly fake kind of blond.

I kept feeling that I ought to know who she was, but I hadn't managed to place her. I decided to try. "Jill, are you here just for the summer?"

"Yes."

"You mentioned that you and Jeremy worked together. Where do you work?"

Jill shot a quick glance at me, then dropped her eyes to the sand. "It's just a summer job," she said. "How long will these guys look for Jeremy before they give up?

"I don't know." Had she just changed the subject? "They won't look for, well, too long. The lake currents make it hard to predict just where . . ."

I stopped. Maybe I'd said enough. "Where are you from, Jill?"

"I'm from Indianapolis. I'm a senior at Northwestern."

"Great school! What's your major?"

I got that under-the-lashes look again. "I'm in the School of Communication."

"Is that journalism?"

"Not exactly." She looked at me. "You're sure there's no way to make a cell phone call from here?"

"No. There's no service on the lakeshore. But I can take you up to my house if you want to make a call."

"It doesn't seem right to leave. But I need to talk to my . . ." She hesitated. "Our boss."

"I'm sure he's heard what happened by now."

"I know!" Jill turned around and stared at the people on top of the bank behind us. "I don't understand why he hasn't come."

The line of volunteers had reached the edge of the water. They dropped their arms and began to talk to one another. Hogan, who was directing the operation, began to gesture to his left, apparently indicating where they would try the next time. Three of the women came over for bottles of water. None of them spoke to Jill, and she didn't look up at them.

Jill and I sat silently until they went back into the water, linking their elbows again and forming a line in a new area. It didn't seem to be a likely spot to me. It was south of the spot where Jill thought Jeremy had gone down. The southwest current should have washed him farther north. But what did I know? Hogan was the expert.

Jill was still drooping. She pulled her knees up to her chest and rested her head on them. It was as if she couldn't stand to look at the water any longer.

I tried to think of something comforting to say. Even though she had denied several times that she had any deep emotional attachment to Jeremy, witnessing something like this had to be upsetting. I was upset, and I'd never met Jeremy. I knew the morning had been a nightmare to Jill.

What could I say to her? My mind was a blank.

Then I heard a woman's voice behind me. "Jill! Lee!"

I pulled myself out of my own four-inch-high chair—an awkward job—and crawled out from under the umbrella. Jill stayed where she was, but she lifted her head.

I looked toward the bank behind us. A woman was standing at the top, behind the yellow no-admittance tape. She was waving a big straw hat. "Lee! Jill! It's me! Maggie."

I walked toward her, and she waved again. "They won't let me through unless you vouch for me!"

It was Maggie McNutt, who had been aboard Joe's Shepherd Sedan the night we were boarded by the pirates.

Before I could do anything to indicate that Maggie should be allowed on the beach, a streak of white terry cloth went by me.

"Maggie! Maggie!" Jill was running up the stairs toward the top of the bank. "I am so glad you're here!"

As Jill ran by, I realized where I'd seen her before, why she had seemed so familiar to me.

Jill was an actress in the Warner Pier Summer Showboat Players. Joe and I had gone to see their production of *Arsenic and Old Lace*. She'd played the romantic lead. According to the posters around town, she was about to open as Mabel in *The Pirates of Penzance*, wearing a cute Victorian bonnet and side curls.

Maggie, of course, was part of the Summer Showboat Players, too, and was in *The Pirates of Penzance*.

As soon as Jill got to the top of the bank, she and Maggie grabbed each other in a big hug. Jill even cried a few tears on Maggie's shoulder.

"Oh, Maggie!" Jill said. "Where is Max?"

"He's gone to Chicago for the day."

"Chicago!" Jill stepped back, her face a picture of incredulity. "He can't have left town!"

"Why not?"

Jill stamped her foot as hard as a flip-flop can be stamped in sand. "The rat! I'll kill him for this!"

Maggie looked confused. She opened her mouth, but before she could say anything, I heard a shout behind us.

"They've found something!"

I lifted the yellow tape and let Maggie through before I bothered to turn around. We'd already had several such announcements. So far the beach patrol had found a log, a sand-filled foam cooler, and a pair of tennis shoes with the laces tied together.

But when I turned around this time, the situation looked different. The searchers in the water were gathered in a tight knot, a knot that was hiding whatever they had found. It was something large.

I had an urge to protect the younger woman, and I guess Maggie did, too, because we both stepped closer to Jill. Maggie put her arm around Jill's waist. We all stared at the scene.

A leg flashed into and out of view. It was horizontal, so I knew it didn't belong to one of the searchers. I gasped, and I think Jill and Maggie did, too. The line of searchers had apparently found Jeremy.

It took the rescue crew only a few minutes to lift the body onto the beach. Hogan stood by with a yellow plastic sheet, which I knew was standard equipment he kept in his car. The searchers closed in, forming a wall that blocked the onlookers' view of the drowned man. Hogan knelt, staying on his knees for at least two full minutes. I wondered why. Then I saw the sheet flap around, and one of the county deputies catch the end. He and Hogan had apparently covered the man.

Hogan stood up and walked up to Maggie, Jill, and me. Silence had fallen over the assembled rescue workers. Hogan stopped about six feet away from us.

"Jill," he said. "I'm sorry, but I have to ask you to identify him."

"This can't be happening," Jill said. Tears were trickling down her cheeks.

"Hogan, I know him, too," Maggie said. "Can I do it?"

"No!" Jill spoke sharply. "I'm not just an ingénue. I've got to act like a grown woman."

She took a deep breath and stepped forward.

"Good girl," Hogan said. He took her arm. They walked toward the water, with Maggie and me following.

The clump of rescuers parted as we approached, and I saw a strange thing. Something was holding the sheet up on the right side of the drowning victim. It looked as if his arm was bent at the elbow and was holding the sheet up like a tent pole. Even as upset as I was, it struck me as odd.

We reached the victim, and Hogan knelt at his head. Maggie again slid her arm around Jill's waist, and I stood close beside her.

Hogan pulled the sheet back. We saw the side of the man's head and a bush of black hair.

"No!" Jill gasped and staggered, nearly falling to her knees. "Jeremy is blond!"

She whirled around and hugged Maggie excitedly. "Jeremy is blond! This isn't him! They've found someone else!"

Chocolate Chat
Chocolate Gives Clue to Ancient Life

Chocolate proves the existence of a vital and important pre-Columbian civilization in the American Southwest.

According to Craig Childs, author of numerous books on archaeology and a commentator on National Public Radio, unusual potsherds were found at a dig in northwestern New Mexico. Reassembled, they became tall, slender pots. What could ancient New Mexicans have used them for?

Similar ones had been found at Mayan sites, and scientists knew the Maya used them for drinking chocolate during ceremonies. But cacao doesn't grow in New Mexico. Too dry. Too far north.

Then the residue found on the potsherds was analyzed. It contained theobromine. Theobromine is found only in chocolate.

The ancient inhabitants of the desert Southwest had used those pots exactly as the Maya did—for a bitter, grainy drink made from cacao beans.

That chocolate must have reached them through a trading route that would have stretched more than a thousand miles south. Add this evidence of international trade to their elaborate building projects—large towns and well-engineered waterways—and Childs says we can't picture pre-Columbian Native Americans living a primitive life. They had a sophisticated civilization. Archaeologists have long known this, but that chocolate was the final proof.

Chapter 5

That sure got everybody's attention.

The beach buzzed. The search team had found the wrong drowning victim? How could that be?

Who could it be?

Maggie quickly leaned over to check out the dead man, looking at his hair as Jill had, then at his face. She nodded at Hogan. "Jill is right. That's not Jeremy."

"We'll check to make sure no one else is missing in the area," Hogan said.

Maggie frowned. "If another drowning had been reported . . ."

"Yeah," Hogan said. "We'd probably have heard."

I realized that Hogan was one of the few people on the beach who hadn't looked surprised by the discovery that the dead man was not Jeremy. He looked serious, but he wasn't amazed the way the rest of us were. I looked at the body myself—like Jill, I skipped the face—and I began to put a few things together. Such as the dead man's arm, the one holding the sheet up like a tent pole. The stiffness looked like rigor mortis to me. However, Jeremy had supposedly been in the water for just a couple of hours. I didn't think that was long enough for rigor mortis to develop. I could be wrong, since I know little about medical matters, but Hogan had formerly served as a homicide detective, so he'd seen plenty of bodies.

Hogan marshaled his line of marching volunteers for another sweep through the water, still looking for Jeremy, then took Jill aside for what looked like an in-depth questioning session. Maggie and I sat down in the beach chairs under the umbrella. Maybe this was my chance to find out what Maggie knew about Jeremy and Jill.

"Just who is this Jeremy?" I said.

"He's on the tech crew at the theater."

"Then I haven't seen him onstage?"

"Nope. Though he's a good-looking guy. I was a little surprised that he was more interested in the backstage angle of theater. Usually the good-looking guys want to be out front."

"Is he a student?"

"I don't think so. He works backstage in Chicago theaters."

"Jill says she's a student at Northwestern. I guess I thought most of the people working at the Showboat this summer were students."

"Most of the actors are. Crew—maybe half and half. Then there are a few of us elderly types." She was being ironic. We both think the early thirties is young, though the student actors Maggie had been working with might not.

"Why do you care?" Maggie said.

"My usual curiosity. I'm just trying to get the picture."

"Picture of what?"

"Of Jill, I guess. Is she as flaky as she seems?"

Maggie shot me a look that could only be described as hostile. "Aren't all actresses supposed to be flaky?"

Her question surprised me. Maggie and I had been buddies for two years. Was she taking my remark personally? I didn't want to fight with her, and I certainly hadn't intended to put down her profession.

"I don't know about all actresses, Maggie," I said. "I certainly don't consider you flaky. You're one of the most levelheaded people I know."

"Now I am." Maggie sounded bitter. She ducked her head and dug up a handful of sand, then let it trickle through her fingers. "God knows I spent years of my life being flaky."

"At least you didn't get married when you were still at the flaky stage, the way I did. I'm sorry if I seemed judgmental about Jill. She's no sillier than I was at her age."

Maggie and I both stared across the beach at Jill and Hogan. Hogan was frowning down at the girl. His face was grim. Jill was twisting a lock of her hair like a ten-year-old. Somehow her mouth looked as if she had developed a lisp. As we watched, she ducked her head and looked up at Hogan from under her lashes. She was behaving like a little girl.

"Yuck," Maggie said. "This is not the way Jill usually acts. Flaky is too kind a word."

"You think it's all an act?"

Maggie gave me another sharp look. "'Act' as in acting? So if actors aren't flaky, they're phony?"

"Come on, Maggie! I just think she's behaved oddly. I'd like to know why."

"What did she do that's so odd?"

"For one thing, she refused to tell me that she's an actor."

I repeated the exchange in which Jill had told me she was "in the School of Communication."

Maggie looked troubled. But she still apparently felt that she had to stick up for her fellow theater employee.

"Okay!" she said. "I admit it was an odd answer. I can't explain it. You'll just have to ask Jill herself."

With that, Maggie got up, pulled herself to her full five feet two inches, and walked over toward Jill and Hogan. Hogan waved her off, however, and she veered toward the water. She ducked her head and walked along, examining the rocks along the wave line. Or pretending to.

In a few minutes Hogan gave up on questioning Jill, and she came back to the umbrella. "Yeesh!" she said as she dropped into the beach chair Maggie had vacated. "Is that police chief always like that?"

"Like what?"

"Having to have every little thing explained to him."

"That's his job. Understanding all the details builds the big picture. What did he want to know?"

"The same old stuff. Why Jeremy and I came here. Exactly what happened when he went under."

Jill went back to her dispirited pose—knees against her chest, head drooping, shoulders slumped, fingers trailing in the sand.

"I'm just tired of going over it," she said.

I was tired of the whole thing, too. Maybe that's what made me bring up another question, one that had been circling around the back of my brain for most of the morning.

"Jill," I said, "just why did you run to our house this morning?"

She didn't look up, but her body became more alert. It

was as if an alarm had gone off, as if I'd yelled, "Watch out!" instead of asking a simple question.

I didn't repeat the question, but after a pause Jill spoke. "I went to your house because I needed help."

"Yes, but why did you come to Joe and me for it?"

Now I got a sideways glance from behind Jill's sunglasses. It was a quick glance. Immediately her eyes dropped back to the sand.

"You were the first person I saw," she said. "You were there."

"Yep, Joe and I were there. But you ran past five houses to get to us."

"I didn't see anybody at those houses."

"Weren't there cars in the drives?"

"Maybe. I don't remember."

"Television sets playing? Lights on? Coffee perking?"

"I don't know!"

We were both silent. Then Jill took a deep breath. "I guess I panicked."

"Did you yell for help before you saw me?"

"I don't remember!"

"It just seems odd, Jill. There are houses within calling distance of this beach, houses you had to run by to get to our mailbox. Joe and I are sort of far from the beach to be first responders for a drowning accident."

Jill jumped to her feet. "I don't have to take this! I don't even have to stay here. I'll tell that Chief Jones that I'm leaving. I can go back to my room. I'll find my boss."

"Max?"

"Mr. Morgan. He'll help me deal with you locals!"

She began snatching up her belongings. Beach towel and

sunscreen were stuffed into a bag. She yanked my terry-cloth cover-up off and threw it down on the chair she'd been sitting in.

"I don't think they'll let you take Jeremy's car," I said. "Do you want me to give you a ride?"

"No! Maggie will take me."

She dropped her bag and walked swiftly down the beach toward Maggie, calling out her name. I remained where I was, sitting in my beach chair while Jill talked to Maggie, then reported to Hogan. When she and Maggie came back, Jill didn't speak. She picked up her beach bag without looking at me.

"Jill," I said, "if Max Morgan is mixed up in this, you can't blame me for wondering if it's some kind of a publicity stunt."

She kept her head turned away from me. "If I've gone through a day like today for a publicity stunt, we'll have another dead man," she said. "And his name will be Max Morgan."

She and Maggie left.

She'd summed up my feelings. If I'd gone through a day like today for a stunt to publicize the Warner Pier Summer Showboat Playhouse, I might murder Max Morgan myself.

But looking for one body and finding another—well, it didn't seem like a coincidence either.

In fact, how could Jeremy's disappearance be a publicity stunt at all? Why would it get publicity? To be blunt, people drown in Lake Michigan every year. I'm afraid they're rapidly forgotten by the general public. Only their friends and relatives remember.

Jeremy's disappearance seemed more like an escape plan. Could he be fleeing from justice? Or from his landlord? Or from some other threat? Obviously, if Jeremy's body didn't turn up, Hogan would be looking into that angle.

And who was this other guy, the one whose body *had* turned up? Losing Jeremy at Beech Tree Public Access Area and finding a completely different person was weird. Hogan was going to be looking for a logical explanation for that, too.

The whole thing was strange. I did think that Jill had deliberately come to Joe and me for help. Our house was too far from the beach for her simply to stumble over us. In the winter, when most of the houses along Lake Shore Drive are empty—maybe it made sense. You could walk a mile, knocking on every door, and not find anybody home. But in the summer, on a weekend, when all the cottages were rented to summer people or occupied by their owners—it just wasn't likely.

I needed to talk to Hogan about it. And he was too busy to talk.

I also needed to discuss the situation with Joe. Maybe he'd see some logical reason for Jill to have approached us.

I hoped so. But for the moment, I thought I was right. And if I was right, the next person to talk to was Max Morgan. After all, both Jill and Jeremy worked for him. He should know something about them.

And Max might be in Chicago for the day, but I had his cell phone number. He'd called me from it repeatedly during the time he was frantically trying to find the pirates, so I had finally stored it in my cell phone so I could call him back easily.

Of course, Max's phone number was no use to me at the beach. The lakeshore is out of reach of all cell phone towers. I'd have to go to the house, where I could look the phone number up on my cell phone, then use our landline to call him. I resolved to do that ASAP.

I looked around the beach. Jill and Maggie had left. There were plenty of people around to keep an eye on the police department's cooler. I could go home.

I stood up and folded up the big umbrella. I shook the sand out of the two beach towels we'd laid out; then I rolled them up. I stuffed them and the beach cover-up Jill had worn into my tote bag. I was folding up one of the squatty beach chairs when Hogan called to me.

He'd been near the body of the unknown man while the EMTs loaded it into a body bag. Now he walked across the sand toward me.

"Lee, would you mind hanging around a few more minutes?"

"Of course, Hogan. I'll stay all day, if you need me. But after Jill left . . ."

Hogan nodded. "I know. I appreciated your sitting with her. But there's one other thing I wanted to ask you and Joe about."

"What's that?"

"Let's wait until Joe is out of the water."

The line of searchers was nearing the water's edge again. Joe looked grim. He loves swimming, but this wasn't swimming. It's no fun to feel around—well, it's no fun. He wore a T-shirt, a ball cap, and sunglasses, but his arms still looked as if he'd gotten too much sun. All the volunteers looked equally tired.

Suddenly I could have wrung Jill's neck. If Jeremy hadn't drowned, if this was some sort of stunt, if she'd put those volunteers and Hogan and his officers and the sheriff's deputies through a miserable day . . . I growled.

Hogan motioned Joe over.

"Listen," he said, "I want you and Lee to check something out before they take this body away."

A little shiver went down my back. I guess it was visible, because Joe reached over and took my hand. "Lee might not want to do that," he said.

"I'm tough enough to take it," I said. "I know Hogan has a good reason or he wouldn't ask."

"It's not gruesome," Hogan said.

He led us over to the body bag and unzipped it so that it uncovered the shoulder of the drowned man. The man wore a short-sleeved blue T-shirt.

Hogan pushed the sleeve back and pointed at what was underneath.

"Does that seem familiar?"

On the man's upper arm was a tattoo—a tattoo of a skull and crossbones.

Joe gasped, but I was the one who spoke.

"Oh, my gosh!" I said. "He must be one of the pirates!"

Chapter 6

Joe reached down and unzipped the body bag to reveal the entire length of the drowned man.

"I guess I'd better look at him more carefully," he said.

I decided I'd better be brave and look, too, but the effort turned out not to require much courage. He didn't look shocking.

"How tall would you say he is?" I said.

"Over six feet," Hogan answered. "We don't have an exact measurement yet."

Joe frowned. "I guess he could have been the larger pirate, the one who came aboard first."

"The pirate's beard, of course, was obviously fake," I said. "But I doubt he would have pasted on extra chest hair. Is his chest furry?"

Hogan peeked under the blue tee and nodded.

"His hair is the right color," I said. "Or at least it's the color of the hair we could see peeking out from under that bandana. Are his hands callused?"

"Like an acrobat?" Joe checked. "Well, he has calluses, but he might be a ditch digger."

I stepped back, suddenly remembering my suspicion about Jill, the idea I'd had that she had deliberately sought Joe and me out after Jeremy disappeared. Maybe this was the time to talk to Joe and Hogan about that, if I could get their attention. They were still staring at the dead man.

"Okay, y'all," I said. "I have a strange idea, and I want to lay it on the two of you."

They listened to my deductions without comment, allowing me to come to the end and sum them up.

"I think Jill deliberately ran down Lake Shore Drive and intercepted me," I said. "I don't know if she would have run up to the house to find Joe or me, or if somebody gave her a signal, so she could run up at exactly the moment when I walked out to the road to get the paper. But I'm convinced that she came to Joe and me on purpose."

Neither Joe nor Hogan told me my idea was a dumb one, so I took it one step further. "What I don't understand is why. Why would Jill want to come to us rather than any of our neighbors?"

I gestured toward the body bag. "And if this guy was one of the pirates, why was Joe's boat the first one boarded? Could that be a coincidence? It doesn't sound likely to me."

I turned to Hogan. "So please don't try to tell me this guy—Captain Blood or whoever he is—just *happened* to drown right off our beach."

Joe spoke then. "Did he drown at all?"

"We don't know yet," Hogan said. "I'm not guessing until after the autopsy."

"I wasn't at the end of the line where they found him," Joe said. "But it looked as if he was—well, caught on the bottom some way."

Hogan nodded. "A log was holding him down."

"It could have been an accident, then."

"Right."

"But nobody else has been reported missing?"

"Nope. No other drownings have been reported anywhere on the lake this week. And that doesn't necessarily have any meaning either."

Joe nodded. "Right. If the guy was out by himself, it's all too easy for a boat to go down and not be missed. Same deal with a lone swimmer. But the members of this rescue team are the kind of people who hang out around the beaches and marinas, and none of them seemed to recognize this guy."

"Nope. But he might not be from Warner Pier."

I jumped back into the conversation. "You've been around a lot of downing cases, Hogan. How long do you think he had been in the water?"

"I'm not an expert, but I'd guess ten or twelve hours. Maybe a little longer."

"Since last night?"

"I could be completely wrong." Hogan motioned to the ambulance crew. "I guess that's all we can do until the autopsy. And until he's identified."

The ambulance took the unknown man's body away, and Hogan called the searchers out of the water. If Jeremy Mattox was in the water in that area, he would stay there until he floated up. That could happen anywhere up and down the lakeshore, but I decided I wouldn't be doing any swimming at Beech Tree Public Access Area for a few days. In fact, I went home and took a shower, and I hadn't even been in the water.

I had to spend some time on the phone, of course. Aunt Nettie wanted to know what was going on, and so did Brenda, though I could tell Tracy had put her up to calling. Brenda simply isn't a professional gossip, compared to Tracy. At least Brenda had learned that. She was still being closemouthed about how her romance with Will was going. Tracy kept trying to pump *me* to find out.

After lunch—we didn't eat until after one thirty—Joe went out, saying he was going to do some errands.

As soon as he left, I dug out my cell phone and found Max Morgan's cell phone number. Then I sat down with a yellow pad and made some notes about what to ask him.

Who was Jeremy? Where had he come from? Why had he been hired?

Plus, what did he have to do with Joe and me?

I also gave some thought to the fact that I hadn't told Hogan I was planning to call Max. But why should he care? No crime appeared to have been committed, unless Jill could be charged with making a false report of a drowning. I wasn't sure what crime that would be, but it sounded illegal.

With my thoughts organized, I punched in Max's number.

I didn't really expect him to answer. After all, he was supposedly in Chicago. He was probably in a meeting. If he was smart, he'd have his phone turned off. I'd have to leave a number.

But the phone rang only once before Max's voice resonated in my ear.

"Lee?"

I felt a bit surprised at his greeting, even though I knew his cell phone would tell him who was calling.

"Max, I have a couple of questions for you. Is this a bad time?"

"No, I'm fine. What can I do for you?"

"I guess you've heard about Jeremy Mattox."

"Have they found him?"

"They gave up about an hour and a half ago."

Max answered, but his words seemed to be meant more for himself than for me. "Seems like they didn't try too long."

"I don't know what the rules are, Max. But when a victim isn't in the immediate area where he went down, they wait a day or two and start a different sort of search."

"Yeah, I get it. How's Jill? They said you were with her."

"She went home."

"What about this guy they did find?"

I described the man with the tattoo. "Does he sound familiar?" I said.

"No. Believe me, if I'd noticed a skull and crossbones tattoo on anybody, I'd have gotten acquainted with him."

Max kept talking, but this time I shut him up. "Max! I called because I have a few questions for you."

"Oh?"

"Tell me about Jeremy."

"What's to tell? He's a great tech. I was lucky to get him. Losing him would be a serious matter."

"How did you find him?"

"Through the grapevine. I put out the word in the Chicago theater crowd, and he called me. His résumé looked good. He needed work for the summer. I hired him."

"Was he easy to work with? Popular with the rest of your people?"

Max gave a short laugh. "Apparently he was popular with Jill. But, yeah, he seemed to get along with everybody."

"He's not from around here originally, is he?"

"Not that I know of. Actually, I don't know where he grew up. Why?"

"I just wondered whether he was local. Has he shown any particular interest in Joe and me?"

"In Joe and you? Why would he do that?"

"That's what I'm trying to figure out. Did he?"

"Not in my hearing."

This wasn't leading anywhere. I thought a moment.

Max spoke again. "Why do you want to know all this?"

"It's hard to explain. What do you think of Jeremy?"

"I don't think anything much of him. He's just a tech, Lee! I've got twenty-five people to handle over there at the Showboat."

"So he didn't stand out in any way?"

"Not to me. He did his job. Seemed to know his business. What did you think of him?"

"I've never met him."

"Sure you have. He came in the shop with me."

"He did?" I quit talking and thought for a moment. "Not that—that blond guy!"

"That's him."

When I heard that, I nearly hung up. I wanted to sink through the floor. Jeremy Mattox, I realized, had been a witness to one of my most embarrassing moments. Remembering it, I was again filled with extreme humiliation.

I've always been afflicted with malapropism. Malapropism is named for Mrs. Malaprop, a character in an eighteenth-century play by Richard Brinsley Sheridan. She is famous, according to *Bartlett's Familiar Quotations*, for saying things such as, "As headstrong as an allegory on the banks of the Nile." Like her, I use the wrong word, usually one that sounds like the correct word, though I don't think I've ever mixed up "allegory" and "alligator." In fact, I can usually remember that they have crocodiles on the Nile, and alligators in the Everglades.

But I frequently get my "tang tongled," the way I did when I told Brenda I considered her my babysitter.

Once I asked my economics professor to remember his own undergrad days and grade my final exam with "apathy." I meant "empathy," of course. Luckily, he thought my mistake was funny. Or I guess it was lucky. He told the story all over the department, but he gave me an A.

I admit that my mistakes can be funny—to other people—and they usually happen only when I'm nervous. So I try to correct them and go on as if I hadn't said something really stupid.

But I try not to make them insulting.

The episode Max was talking about had happened during the time when he was hounding me to identify the pirates who had boarded our boat.

He had come into the shop yet one more time, and he and I were sitting in my office. He was again quizzing me about each of the pirates.

"One of the guys was tall," I said. "The other wasn't. The girl had a sexy figure. Really, Max! I don't know what else to tell you. They were covered with wigs and makeup. None of them had a wooden leg or one blue eye and one brown or anything else obvious."

It was at this point that the door to the shop opened, and someone came in. Both the counter girls had gone to the back, so I stood up and leaned out the door of my office, looking toward the workroom to make sure one of them was coming up to wait on the new customer, but I kept talking to Max, and I didn't really look at the customer.

"Why are you so fixated on this?" I said.

"Because of *The Pirates of Penzance*."

"Surely you've got an actor ready to play the Pygmy King," I said.

Okay. I meant the Pirate King, one of the biggest and most colorful roles in *The Pirates of Penzance*. I'd twisted my tongue, as usual.

That wouldn't have been bad.

But as I said it, I turned away from Max and found myself—well, I can't say face-to-face; it would have to be chest-to-face—with the man who'd just come in the door.

He was barely five feet tall.

Of course, since I'm just a shade less than six feet tall, I was towering over him.

He looked at me, deadpan, with his head tipped slightly back. I stared at him. I could feel my face growing hot. And I began to stammer.

"The Pirate King!" I said. "I mean the Pirate King! I'm sure you have an actor for that role. After all, the short must go on."

I didn't try to correct that one. I simply slunk back to my chair and collapsed.

Max had snickered. I remember that. Then he spoke to the man who had come in, and I realized the short guy had come in to see Max. Max may have introduced us. I don't remember. The blood was pounding in my ears, and the office was spinning.

The man spoke to Max, making a rather odd comment. "I've got the ice bucket set up," he said.

The comment seemed to annoy Max, who said, "I thought we were taking the cooler."

The short man frowned, shrugged, and left.

I remembered the episode, but it was my embarrassment that stuck in my mind, not the man who had come into the shop. Now I tried to remember him.

He was blond, as Jill had said. He was probably less than an inch over five feet tall, but he was well proportioned. Well, sort of. Actually, his shoulders were too broad, so his physique was somewhat odd. But broad shoulders are not something men complain about. I remember he was wearing a T-shirt and khaki shorts—the Warner Pier uniform—and his tee was tight enough to show off smooth muscles. He might have been small, but he looked macho. I couldn't remember his face, but I remembered that he wasn't unattractive. I could see that Jill might well have been attracted to him.

Now I recalled my attention to my phone call. Max told me he would be heading for Warner Pier within the hour and assured me he'd check on Jill when he got there. She lived, he told me, in the small dorm the theater ran for cast and crew members.

I somehow found my voice and said good-bye. Then I hung up, and I again tried to picture Jeremy Mattox. Something about his appearance was trying to bubble up from my memory.

I went into the kitchen and stared out the window, and I tried to remember. His face? I couldn't describe it in detail. His build? Muscular, but not muscle-bound. His clothing?

As I said, Jeremy had worn the Warner Pier uniform, khaki shorts and a T-shirt. I was wearing the same thing myself at that moment—my polo shirt was a medium blue. I don't know why khaki shorts are the standard garb for our town, but they are. The only variation for summer workers comes in the colors of their T-shirts. City employees wear white, for example, and TenHuis counter girls, naturally, wear chocolate brown.

T-shirt. I closed my eyes and pictured Jeremy Mattox. His T-shirt had been a reddish orange, a rather odd color. And it had words across the front.

What did the T-shirt say?

Suddenly I remembered.

"Camp Sail-Along."

Chapter 7

It was the distinctive red-orange color that tickled my memory and made me recall the words on the shirt.

Warner Pier is in summer camp country, of course. All around us are church camps, sports camps, math or science camps—like the one where Ken McNutt was teaching—and those camps where rich parents park their kids for the entire summer. Some of the camps are old, some new. But Camp Sail-Along's shirt was recognizable because it wasn't a standard red, blue, green, or yellow. It was that color sometimes called "bittersweet" or maybe "brick," a bright rust that might be hard to find in an ordinary T-shirt catalog. On the shirt's left front was a triangular logo that seemed to represent a sail. The name was centered under the logo.

Apparently Camp Sail-Along was a sailing camp. But it could be either a day camp or a residential camp.

What connection could Jeremy Mattox have had with Camp Sail-Along? Maybe none. The camp might have sold some leftover shirts at a garage sale, and he picked one up for a couple of bucks. Or he could have been a counselor there sometime. Or he could have had a girlfriend who was a counselor there. Or he could have been a camper there, once upon a time.

I decided to find out more about the camp. I called the secretary of the Warner Pier Chamber of Commerce, Zelda Gruppen. I had to begin by apologizing for bothering her on her afternoon off.

"It's okay," she said. "I'm just doing laundry. Any interruption is welcome. What can I do for you?"

"Do you know anything about Camp Sail-Along?"

"I know they got new ownership and dropped their chamber membership."

"Dirty deal! Why'd they do that?"

"I only talked to one guy, and he was quite friendly, but he wasn't very informative. I think his name was Jack. I'd have to look at the files to tell you any more."

"Was Jack the new owner?"

"I couldn't figure out if he was the owner or the manager or maybe the handyman. All I know is that I sent a statement for their annual dues, and I didn't get a reply. So I phoned the old number. This Jack answered and said they weren't going to join this year. He said it was going to be a 'restructuring' year."

"Hmm. So they left the door open for future membership." I mulled the situation over.

"Yeah," Zelda said, "but I didn't feel hopeful when I hung up. Why do you need to know?"

"It's kind of complicated." I made up my mind. "Do you have any membership material handy? I don't want to send you back to the office, but I could make a membership call on them this afternoon."

"Why? I mean, what's the attraction?"

"I got curious about the camp. A membership call will give me an excuse to take a look at it. And maybe they'll rejoin."

"Good luck with that! And I think you'll need it. I've got some brochures in my car, and you can have them. I'm not going to turn down an offer of a volunteer membership call."

Thirty minutes later I had put on sandals, sage green slacks, and an ivory cotton sweater—dress-up business attire for Warner Pier—had picked up a dozen membership brochures from Zelda, and was headed for Camp Sail-Along.

I'd had to look up the address. It wasn't inside the Warner Pier city limits, of course. It was a mile inland on a small body of water called Lake o' the Winds. The entrance to the camp was off McIntosh Road and was marked by a dilapidated sign. I got a sinking feeling when I saw it. I had speculated that Jeremy Mattox might have picked up a shirt at a garage sale, and now I saw a notice attached to the main Camp Sail-Along sign. That notice said YARD SALE.

Oh, gee! My speculation had come true, and my trip was looking like a washout. But I didn't turn back. I laughed at my lucky guess and drove on.

The driveway curved through a band of trees and came out on a sunny lawn. Eight or ten cabins were grouped around a larger building, a building with a broad porch. It was the classic summer camp layout: cabins used as bunkhouses and a central building for meals.

Only two other vehicles were in the parking lot—a rattletrap pickup and a subcompact. This yard sale was following the typical pattern of such events—the serious shoppers had come early. By late afternoon, the sale was dragging to a close.

The yard sale was set up on the porch of the main building. A guy in white was standing behind the table, apparently running the sale, and I could see that he was in trouble. The woman across from him was Lovie Dykstra.

Lovie was a well-known Warner Pier character. She had a special liking for me because—long ago—my mother was engaged to her younger son. When the son died, my mom left town and wound up in Dallas, where she married a long, tall Texan who became my dad. But Lovie says I was almost her granddaughter, and no matter how far-fetched her idea is, she treats me like a relative.

Her personal troubles drove Lovie out of her original career, teaching, and today Lovie is a secondhand dealer. She still has unruly gray hair, but a year and a half ago Lovie's life took a turn for the better, and today she's known as a town character, rather than the town crazy woman.

Lovie will buy or sell anything. And she drives a hard bargain.

I took pity on the camp representative and walked toward the porch. I surmised that he'd had a long, lonely day. He had a radio to keep him company. It was tuned to a fifties station.

As I approached, I heard Lovie's raspy voice. "I'll take everything that's left, take it right off your hands."

I looked at the items left on the table. If I'd been the short guy, I'd have snapped up twenty-five dollars. The things left looked like junk to me. Towels were stacked neatly, but the top one was stained, and they all had frayed edges. A box of silverware was beside them, and all the forks seemed to have bent tines. Ragged blankets, some rusty skillets, a box of leather scraps, odd lengths of rope, and, yes, a dozen or so T-shirts in a bright rust color were also on the table. A cardboard card propped against the tees read, "$1."

Thin, worn mattresses were piled at the end of the porch, and pillows were heaped on a second table.

Lovie was facing the table with hands on hips. The man in white laughed. He was on the short side, but he had unusually broad shoulders, medium brown hair, and a flirty mustache. "I couldn't possibly sell you all this stuff for twenty-five," he said. "It's worth several hundred at least."

"To the right person, maybe," Lovie said. "But you don't want to stand around here until the right person comes along. You want to move it, right? Think of the time my offer will save you! Time's money."

"My time's not worth much. Give me two hundred and fifty, and I'll think about it."

Lovie rolled her eyes. "Don't be silly! What are you going to get for those mattresses? Nothing. They'll go for scrap, but nobody will show up at a yard sale to take them."

Lovie had a point. I smiled at the man, and he smiled back. In fact, I got the whole treatment—every tooth in his head. Then I spoke. "Hi, Lovie."

She turned toward me and beamed. "Lee! Honey!" We hugged each other. "Now, Lee," she said, "you tell this fellow that I know my business."

"That's for darn tootin', Lovie. But I'm staying out of this. I'll just see what size these T-shirts are."

I dug through the stack of bittersweet-colored tees, looking for one the size of somebody I knew. Lovie and the camp man haggled. She raised her bid to fifty dollars, but they hadn't reached a deal when Lovie walked off and got into her beat-up truck.

She leaned out the window and hollered at me before she drove away. "Come see me, Lee! You and Joe!"

I waved at her, then grinned at the Camp Sail-Along man. "You accomplished something today. You met one of Warner Pier's real characters."

"Oh, I met her yesterday. She checked us out early. Offered me one fifty for everything on sale before we opened. I probably would have been smart to accept."

"She drives a hard bargain." I held out a child-sized shirt. It ought to fit some kid I knew. "I'll take this. And I'll introduce myself. I'm Lee Woodyard, and I'm here representing the Warner Pier Chamber of Commerce."

The man looked me up and down, deadpan. He seemed to be considering just how to react to me. Finally he smiled. "Didn't you call earlier?"

"I think our manager did. That's Zelda Gruppen. Zelda is a staff member. I'm on the board." I stuck out my hand in shaking position.

The man touched my hand with his fingers in one of those obnoxious, halfhearted gestures that mimic shaking hands. "I'm Jack McGrath. I'm the manager of Camp Sail-Along."

"Zelda said you called this a 'restructuring' year, Jack."

"We're not going to offer any camp sessions this year." His mustache took on a rakish tilt as he smiled, and he wiggled his eyebrows. He looked as if he were doing a Groucho Marx impression. "I can't even offer you a boat ride. But I could show you around."

"I'd love a tour, but I don't want to take you away from your sale."

Jack McGrath shrugged. "I don't expect much more business."

At first look, Camp Sail-Along appeared deserted and neglected. Dead leaves had blown into piles on the porches. The windows of the small cabins—the bunkhouses—still wore their winter shutters, and their doors were padlocked. The shutters from the main building had been taken off, but they hadn't been stored. They leaned against the side of the building in drunken heaps.

All the buildings needed paint, and the grass hadn't been mowed, but there were lovely trees, and I could see a long dock extending out into the lake. Camp Sail-Along had the potential to be a very nice spot.

"There's a lot of potential here," I said. "You have a lovely view. And the cabins look as if they'd be comfortable."

"They could be."

"What activities do you plan to offer?"

"We're not quite sure yet. And I'm afraid we're not ready to join the local chamber."

"We'll be here when you are ready. Let me give you one of our brochures."

I gave him a brochure and a membership application, talking all the time about the wonderfulness of Warner Pier and the chamber of commerce. I really am on the board, so that was easy.

Jack McGrath took the brochure and continued to look at me with an expression that was becoming a leer. When he offered to continue our tour, I accepted with pleasure, since I wanted a chance to ask him about Jeremy Mattox, but his insinuating smile was making me feel as if I should take my tire iron with me in case I needed to discourage him emphatically.

McGrath kept smiling excessively as he showed me around. The central building, as I'd guessed, had a kitchen designed to serve up sloppy joes and hot dogs. It was shabby and out of date. TenHuis Chocolade has to deal with the health department, so I'm familiar with their requirements, and I spotted four things they wouldn't approve. The dining room was filled with ramshackle chairs and tables. The building had been swept—sometime that summer—but it wasn't clean.

Only one room, one that might have been designed as an office, was in use. McGrath opened the door and leered at me. "My humble abode," he said.

I could see a couple of cots inside, both with sleeping bags on them. One bag was neatly rolled; the other was scrambled as if Jack McGrath had just gotten out of it. The only storage was two footlockers. One was closed, and the other open, with its contents spewing out.

I didn't go inside the room. "If you're having trouble finding contractors, Mr. McGrath, the chamber of commerce might be able to help you."

"Oh?" His answer was noncommittal.

"We have a list of members with an explanation of the services they offer."

Still no response. I headed for the porch, and McGrath followed me outside. He pointed out the badminton court— no net—and the swimming beach—no nothing. The big storage building, he said, held a dozen small boats.

"What kind of boats do you have?"

McGrath gave an expansive wave, taking in all of Lake o' the Winds. "For the advanced sailors, we have access to the Warner River," he said. "And, of course, that leads to the big lake."

He hadn't answered my question about the small boats. Hmm.

McGrath unlocked the padlock on one of the small cabins and showed me the inside. It was a shambles of rusty springs and mouse-nibbled bedding. The only light came from the door he had opened. If the cabins had electricity, it wasn't turned on. The sides were screened, so the cabins could be opened to the outside air when they were in use, but at that moment shutters completely covered the screens. The cabin was dark and musty. I looked in the door and backed away.

McGrath offered to continue the tour, but I declined. I certainly didn't want to see eight more dirty, ramshackle cabins, and I even passed up a peek at the shower house. There was only one. Apparently the camp had been planned for single-sex sessions.

So as McGrath relocked the cabin's padlock, I turned and strolled toward the van. "I certainly appreciate your taking the time to show me around."

"It's been a pleasure, Lee." He twisted his lip once more, making his mustache wriggle.

It was time for the question I'd come to ask. I tried to sound innocent. "Was this the camp where Jeremy Mattox worked?"

McGrath frowned. "Jeremy who?"

"Mattox."

He paused for at least thirty seconds before he went on. "I don't know. I haven't had any other employees this summer, and I wasn't here last year."

McGrath folded his arms and leaned against the van. His shoulders drooped. He was the picture of discouragement.

"In fact, as you may have guessed, this whole project has turned into a flop."

"I'm sorry to hear that, Jack."

"I'm sorry to say it. Actually, my uncle is a retired coach, and he bought the place, then hired me to run it. But he's undercapitalized."

"Oh, dear."

"Oh, yeah. I'm a coach myself. I thought this would be a great summer job—maybe turn into a full-time deal. But the place is far too run-down to open without a major renovation, and my uncle just doesn't have the money to update. And he can't get a loan, on top of the mortgage on the property."

"Oh, gee! Jack, I sympathize completely. When I came to Warner Pier four years ago to work for my aunt at TenHuis Chocolade, I faced the same situation, in a way."

He grinned. "You look prosperous now."

"We're doing better. But for the first two years I lived with my aunt, taking room and board as part of my pay—"

"Same deal with me."

"And my aunt and I both took big salary cuts. Luckily, her plant didn't need an upgrade, but she'd let her deliveries get unreliable, so her business was going downhill fast. It took a lot of work to get the business back on track."

I smiled. "And now I'll make another pitch for the chamber of commerce. We can refer you or your uncle to people who can help. No, we can't give you a loan, but we can put you in touch with groups who help with operations, or with accounting practices. This could make a difference."

Jack nodded glumly. "I'm afraid it's too late for that. I think my uncle is just going to put the property on the market."

"Everything on the water is valuable around here."

"Probably not valuable enough to pay off his mortgage."

I nodded sympathetically. "Thanks for showing me around. I appreciate your sharing your time."

"Time's all I've got." McGrath yawned. "I think the sale's over. I may take a nap. Bed sounds good."

"Yes, it does. It's such a lazy afternoon, I could join you."

It wasn't until McGrath's eyes widened that I realized what I had said.

"I mean . . . a nip sounds good. I mean a nap! I mean, it's a lazy afternoon but I'd better go back to work."

I yanked the van's door open and leaped inside.

McGrath was right beside the van's window, grinning. "All I can offer you is a beer," he said. "But it's cold."

"No, I've got to get out of here. I mean, I need to get home."

McGrath extended his hand in a way that made it hard to refuse. I shook it. He didn't let go. None of that namby-pamby touch of the fingers he'd offered the first time we shook hands. This time I got the full-fledged, strong-guy, macho handshake.

It was almost painful. His palm had rough calluses, for one thing. I pulled my hand away, but it wasn't easy.

"My husband repairs and restores wooden boats," I said. "He'll be interested if you decide to sell your equipment."

"Your husband? I was hoping you were single."

"No. I'm married."

I was still getting the eye contact and the frisky mustache. I kept smiling as I started the motor and backed up. Jack McGrath stepped out of the way so I wouldn't run over his foot. We gave each other friendly waves as I drove off.

I'm used to saying the wrong thing, but I'd really done it that time. I could only hope that I never saw Jack McGrath again as long as I lived.

"Stupid," I said aloud. How could I have made one mistake after another?

All I'd done that afternoon was embarrass myself. I had learned nothing about Jeremy Mattox. He remained a mystery man, and not just because he failed to come up from a surface dive. I still wanted to know whether Jill had deliberately sought Joe and me out when Jeremy disappeared.

But Jill had made it clear she didn't want to talk to me.

Maybe Maggie could help me quiz her. Or maybe Maggie knew some other friends of Jeremy's. I needed to find out.

Chapter 8

I tried Maggie's cell phone, but it was turned off. So I headed for her house, all excited about a new line of questioning. It was something of a letdown when I found out she wasn't home.

Ken was, however. He told me Maggie had taken Jill to her dorm and had told him she planned to stay until the young woman seemed to be okay.

"Max Morgan told me Jill lives at the theater dorm," I said. "But where is that?"

Ken chuckled. "It used to be known as the Riverside Motel."

"Oh, gee! What a lucky bunch of actors!"

"They need to suffer for their art," Ken said. We both laughed.

I drove on to the Riverside, now the Showboat dorm. It's a Warner Pier landmark. Sort of.

Warner Pier may be the quaintest resort on the east shore of Lake Michigan, but our pretty little village still has a few spots that are less than picturesque. The Riverside Motel might head the list.

The Riverside was probably the first motel constructed in west Michigan, I'd guess in the early 1930s. In those days motels were usually a collection of tiny buildings, sometimes styled to imitate English cottages or log cabins or—in the Southwest—adobe houses. I found this out from a series of articles on vernacular architecture run in the local weekly. Warner Pier is nuts on architecture of all types.

The Riverside had begun life as a dozen or so faux boathouses. This effect had been attained by putting a little porch on the front of each cabin and using heavy timber piers, like those used for docks, to delineate the porch corners. I've seen a picture from the 1930s showing the motel porches draped with fishing nets.

So each unit of the Riverside is a little house. The roofs still have the original wide eaves. Parking spaces are between the units. Of course, those parking spaces were designed to hold Model Ts, so they are not big enough for today's full-sized cars, though subcompacts or motorcycles fit nicely.

The itty-bitty boathouses are arranged in a semicircle, and in that early-day picture I saw they were centered around a pond about thirty feet across. At some time the pond had been replaced with a swimming pool.

About 1933 the site may have had a certain charm, but neglect and time had de-charmed it. The little boathouses needed paint, the fishing nets and other cutesy props were long gone, and the imitation pier posts had rotted. The swimming pool was cracked, empty of water, filled with trash, and surrounded by a chain-link fence. I didn't want to imagine what the rooms were like. I could almost guarantee that the décor included sagging mattresses, leaking showers, and stained walls. If the Showboat cast and crew members were smart, they brought their own linens. I wouldn't want to touch a sheet or towel provided by the management.

The motel wasn't even in a very convenient location for the Showboat personnel, since it was on the opposite side of the river from the theater. There is a little ferry, but it was strictly for tourists—foot traffic only—and it quit running long before the final curtain on performance nights.

As I pulled into the motel's drive, I realized that I didn't know where I was going. Who was assigned to which little house? Luckily, there was a sign that read MANAGER outside the structure nearest the street. I parked in front of it.

This little boathouse seemed to be living quarters, rather than an office. A sign on the door said PLEASE KNOCK, so I did. At first I thought no one was going to answer, but I wasn't eager to make the rounds of the motel, rapping on each door, so I stood on the porch, looking around the area for someone else I could quiz. Then I heard footsteps dragging inside, and the door opened.

A bone-thin woman stood in the doorway. Her hair was dyed that dead black that means an amateur job, and it was teased as high as 1968.

"Yes?" Her voice was whiny, and somehow her face looked whiny as well. She had that hollow-jawed look that nineteenth-century pioneers had, the look that meant they'd lost their molars.

"I'm sorry to bother you," I said. "I'm looking for Jill Campbell."

"She's in cottage number three, honey. With Mikki White."

"Thanks." I turned away, then thought of another question. "Did Jeremy Mattox live here? I mean, does he live here?"

To my dismay, tears began to run down the woman's face. "Oh, honey, I'm so upset about his accident."

"Yes, it's terrible."

"It was just yesterday he was out back, practicing. I can't believe he's gone!" Her face screwed up like that of a baby about to wail. But she sounded calm enough when she spoke again. "Had you known Jeremy long?"

"I didn't know him at all, I'm afraid. His accident happened near our house. My husband was part of the rescue team." I didn't want to tell her that I was there simply out of nosiness.

Warner Pier is such a small town. This woman probably knew Aunt Nettie. I decided I'd better act polite. "I'm Lee Woodyard. You may know my aunt, Nettie Jones. I work for her at TenHuis Chocolade."

"Nettie Jones? She wasn't Nettie Vanderheide?"

"Yes, she was. She married my uncle, Phil TenHuis. He died five years ago, and last year she remarried."

"I'm Ella Van Ark. I knew Nettie when we were girls. I just moved back home, got the job managing this place." She pulled out a Kleenex and patted her eye. "And now Jeremy is gone. Such a sweet boy!"

"We mustn't give up hope, Mrs. Van Ark. They haven't found him yet."

"True, true. But we'd better prepare ourselves for the worst." She seemed to relish the prospect, although genuine tears were welling in her eyes. "What the theater will do without him, I don't know."

"I understand he was a key employee." I moved to the edge of the porch. I had come to talk to Jill, not a woman who dyed her hair with shoe polish. Then another question occurred to me. "Did Jeremy have a roommate?"

"At first he did, but Harold moved out the second week in June."

"Harold?"

"Yes. Jeremy and Harold Weldon came at the same time, and they roomed together. Seemed to be old friends. Both worked at the theater. Then all of a sudden Harold came over, paid his rent up, and said he had quit his job and was leaving."

I stopped. This Harold might know more about Jeremy than anyone. "Did he say where he was going?"

"Said he had a new job, and it included room and board. I never saw him around again."

"Harold Weldon? Was that his name?"

"Yes." Mrs. Van Ark sighed deeply. "He and Jeremy used to do their tricks out back of their cottage."

"Tricks?"

"They were wonderful. Harold did the lifts, of course. He was big, you know. Big and strong. Jeremy was—is—small. It was a wonder to see him leap right up onto Harold's shoulders."

"Did they perform at the Showboat?"

"They were good enough to. But they never wanted anybody to see them do their act. They said it was 'under development.'"

My heart was going pitter-patter. Had I found two of the pirates? They certainly sounded like the two guys who had boarded our boat. A big guy and a little guy, both trained acrobats.

I found myself longing for a look at Harold. "You don't know where Harold was working?"

"No! He just said that Jeremy would forward any mail he got. And now Jeremy is gone, too. I don't know what I'll do with the things in his cottage."

I assured Mrs. Van Ark that someone, either the authorities or Max Morgan, would contact Jeremy's family. Then I started toward Boathouse 3. Luckily the numbers were clearly marked on the porches.

As I walked, I thought over what Mrs. Van Ark had said. Jeremy and his roommate had apparently been acrobats. She didn't mention them being expert swimmers, but acrobatics was definitely one of the skills the pirates used. Jeremy and Harold would be strong possibilities as the two male pirates.

Could Harold be the man found drowned that morning? Had Jeremy known his body was near Beech Tree Public Access Area? Had Jeremy faked his own drowning to force a search of the area?

But why not just call the authorities and say, "Hey, my buddy was going swimming alone at Beech Tree beach, and he never came home—maybe we'd better look for him"?

But even if I knew the answer to that question, it wouldn't explain why Jill had been programmed to come to Joe and me for help. What did we have to do with a drowning—either of Jeremy or of Harold?

I was so deep in thought that I had walked onto the porch of Boathouse 3 and had raised my hand to rap on the door before I realized where I was.

I didn't have my questions ready. Besides, I was looking for Maggie, not Jill, and I could see that Maggie's car wasn't there. I turned to go away, but the door swung open and a young woman spoke.

"I'd about given up on you!" Then she did a double take. "Oh! I thought you were my roommate."

The most striking thing about the young woman was that she was looking me in the eye. I'm so tall, I rarely look another woman directly in the eye unless she's standing on a footstool.

This girl was not only tall; she was also attractive, with dark hair and smoky gray eyes. Her figure might have been her only drawback; like lots of us tall girls, she was on the thin side—bony rather than curvy.

I prepared to speak politely and go on my way. "Hi. I'm Lee Woodyard—"

The girl gasped so loudly that I quit talking. "I thought you were a guy!"

"No. I'm a gal. Had you heard my name?"

"Hal talked about you. He was supposed to come by to meet you, but he hasn't showed up."

"I think there's some mistake . . ."

"No, no! I'm sure Woodyard was the name. It's—you know—kinda odd."

"Yes, it's unusual, but—"

"I guess I was just being sexist. I mean, I expected a man." She rolled her eyes. "Dumb me!"

I threw up my hands in a stop-traffic gesture. "Wait a minute! I think we're mixed up."

"I sure was."

"Look, is this where Jill Campbell lives?"

"Yes, but she doesn't have anything to do with it."

"You're right. I'm looking for a woman named Maggie McNutt—"

"Oh, I know Maggie!"

"If you're connected with the Showboat, I'm sure you do. Maggie is a friend of mine. She was supposed to be bringing Jill home. I want to talk to Maggie. She didn't answer her cell phone. So I came over." The girl started to say something else, but by using a gesture that was slightly short of putting my hand over her mouth, I managed to keep her from speaking. "I have nothing to do with Hal."

"But you're supposed to!"

"Why?"

"He said you were going to help him."

"I'll be happy to help Hal any way I can. But right now I need to talk to Maggie. Since she's not here, I'll be on my way."

I turned around and started to walk off the porch.

"Don't leave!" the dark-haired girl almost wailed. "Hal will be really mad if he comes and you're not here!"

I turned back. "I never even heard of Hal. What could he possibly want with me?"

"It was a professional engagement! Hal was ready to pay you."

"Pay me? He wanted chocolate?"

"Chocolate?" Now complete confusion came over the girl's face. "He's a health-food nut. I never saw him eat chocolate."

"Look," I said, "we're obviously talking about two different things. If Hal wants to talk to me, ask him to call TenHuis and ask for Lee."

I started toward my van again, this time determined to get in it and drive away, despite the dark girl, who was following along, yapping at my back like an unruly Great Dane.

But when I turned my back on her and looked at the van, the situation became clear.

Joe's truck was parked next to my van, and he was leaning against the fender, arms folded, watching my approach.

I began to laugh, and I spun around to face the girl.

"I get it! Hal is looking for a lawyer."

Chocolate Chat
Chocolate Makes Moms, Babies Happy

It's long been known that chocolate makes women happy. But scientists have found that if pregnant women eat it, apparently their babies will be happier, too.

Researchers at the University of Helsinki observed three hundred pregnant women. Some ate chocolate daily, and some didn't. The scientists discovered that babies born to women who ate chocolate laughed and smiled more than the babies born to women who didn't eat it.

If women who were stressed ate chocolate, researchers also discovered, their babies were less fearful. Mothers who were stressed but who didn't eat chocolate were apt to have babies who were more fearful.

This study was described in "The People's Pharmacy" column written by Joe and Dr. Teresa Graedon. Other types of candy, they said, did not have this effect.

Chocolate can lower blood pressure, the Graedons point out. It can make blood vessels more flexible and help prevent blood clots.

But if you mix sugar with it—watch out! Then we're talking calories.

Chapter 9

The dark-haired girl stared at me. "Well, duh!" she said. "Why else would Hal call you?"

"If he wanted a lawyer, he wouldn't call me. But he might call my husband." I pointed at Joe. "Come on, and I'll introduce you to the attorney in the family."

Joe, the tall girl, and I met beside the fence surrounding the swimming pool. The girl was, as I'd suspected, Jill's roommate, Mikki White.

"Boy, do I feel dumb," she said.

I assured her that she'd made a logical mistake. "You were expecting a lawyer named Woodyard, and when someone by that name showed up, you naturally assumed I was the person you were waiting for. But I'm in the chocolate business. It's just a coincidence that I came by looking for Maggie McNutt."

"But she's not here. And neither is Jill. Hal didn't show up either, and he said he'd be here at four o'clock."

I had belatedly remembered that Hal was a nickname for Harold. "Is Hal the guy Mrs. Van Ark called Harold Weldon?" I said.

"Sure."

I turned to Joe. "He was Jeremy's roommate, but he moved out early in the summer."

"I see." Joe spoke to Mikki. "Why did Hal want to see me?"

"I don't know. He just called and said he needed a place to talk to you and asked if Jill and I would let him use our room."

"I have an office. I wonder why he didn't want to see me there."

Mikki's eyes got as wide as the sky over Lake Michigan. "He didn't want to wait until Tuesday."

That was logical. Since Joe works only three days a week, he wasn't scheduled to have any office appointments until Tuesday.

Mikki kept talking. "Hal was real anxious to talk to you. I can't figure out why he's not here."

I had thought of a reason. Hal, according to his landlady, was tall and acrobatic. I was still wondering whether he was the drowned man found at Beach Tree beach.

I spoke before Joe could, blurting out my question. "Does Hal have a tattoo? On his upper arm?"

Mikki looked at me as if I were crazy. "Not that I know of. I mean, he could. I've never seen him without his shirt. We're not on that sort of terms."

Joe grinned. "What does he look like, Mikki?"

"He's tall. Dark hair. His eyes are really big. He has a heavy beard. I mean, he shaves, but he always has a five o'clock shadow. Why do you need to know?"

"I thought maybe I knew him. I'm trying to figure out why he wanted to talk to me."

"I can tell you what he said. It sounded kind of funny."

"What was it?"

"He said he didn't want to do the time unless he did the crime."

I'm sure I gaped, but Joe nodded as if he understood what Mikki was talking about. Did he? Or was he merely doing his imperturbable-lawyer act?

A crime? If Hal was mixed up in a crime, yes, he probably needed a lawyer, so a call to Joe or some other attorney would be logical. But what sort of a crime could be involved? I'd been standing around becoming more and more sure that Hal was one of the elusive pirates. But that was no crime. Well, maybe if the law wanted to get technical, boarding a boat without permission was a form of burglary. But it was much on a par with trick-or-treaters coming to the door, since no harm was done, and it would be strange for the boat owner to call the cops. I hadn't heard of any boater who had objected to being boarded. They had bragged about it.

No, if Hal was worried about a crime, it probably had nothing to do with our funny summer pirates. But in the last fifteen minutes—ever since Ella Van Ark had told me Hal was an acrobat—I'd become convinced that he must be the drowning victim who had been found at Beech Tree Public Access Area.

While I was analyzing all this, Joe had been quizzing Mikki. No, Hal hadn't said anything that would make his cryptic comment more intelligible. Yes, she had asked him, but he had refused to explain further. He just said he needed a place to meet with Joe.

"I was surprised when he called," Mikki said. "I mean, we're not that close."

Joe's voice was noncommittal. "You don't see him regularly?"

"No, no! He quit his job at the theater. We're just buddies. Pals. We have a lot of repertoire."

It took me a second to realize she meant "rapport." Darn! Mikki was another Mrs. Malaprop, a dark-haired version of me. It was crazy.

After a few more minutes, Joe and I said good-bye to Mikki, and Joe gave her his cell phone number, so she could pass it on to Hal if he showed up. Then Mikki headed toward her room, and Joe turned toward our vehicles. I grabbed his arm.

"Wait a minute! Joe, I can't help wondering if Hal isn't the dead man the rescue team found this morning."

Joe frowned, and I went on before he could speak. "Think about it, Joe! He's tall! He knew Jeremy well. He needs a lawyer, so he's in some kind of trouble. And you haven't heard the most important evidence."

"What's that?"

"He's an acrobat!" I quickly sketched what Ella Van Ark had said about Hal and Jeremy doing their "tricks."

"Don't you think Hogan should ask Mikki to take a look at the body?"

"I don't think she needs to bother, Lee."

"Why not? Have they identified the man?"

"Not that I know of. But Mikki knew Hal because he worked at the Showboat Theater."

"So?"

"Maggie and Jill both worked there, too. And they looked at the body. And they both said they had never seen the man before."

I went to my van completely deflated.

Plus, I still hadn't found Maggie McNutt. I pulled out my

cell phone and called her again. It seemed like a miracle when she answered.

I probably sounded desperate. "Where are you?"

"At the Showboat. I'm sorry I didn't check my messages earlier. I took Jill to get something to eat. By then it was so late, I just dropped her at the theater."

I knew Maggie didn't have a role in that week's production. "Are you going home?"

"Yes. Is something wrong?"

"I'm not sure. But I sure would like to talk to you. Could you meet me at the office?"

"If you'll give me a Mexican vanilla truffle."

"I'll have one with you."

"I'll stop by the Coffee House."

When I got to the office, Will was standing on the sidewalk outside. "Hi, Lee," he said. "Just waiting for Brenda."

I glanced at my watch. "Fifteen minutes before the shift changes."

"We're going into Holland to a movie."

"Have fun." I went in meditating—not for the first time—on how starting the summer with a big fight had made Brenda even more attractive to Will than she had been. He was dancing attendance much more avidly than he had the previous year. Hmm. Not that I'd recommend a tricky move like picking a fight as a ploy that might possibly increase a guy's interest. Honesty remains the best policy. But hmm again.

Ten minutes later Maggie and I were in my glass-walled office, with the door shut against the noise of the tourists in the retail shop. A paper plate was on the desk between us. It held two Mexican vanilla truffles ("light vanilla interior formed into a ball and encased in milk chocolate"), two double-fudge bonbons ("layers of milk and dark chocolate fudge with a dark chocolate coating"), and a half dozen pastilles of dark chocolate with outlines of pirate treasure chests molded into their tops. The plate was flanked by Maggie's contribution, coffees from the Coffee House. Of course, we could have drunk coffee from the TenHuis break room, but the Coffee House has a blend of dark roast that Maggie and I both like plain and black. The bitter flavor was perfect with any kind of chocolate.

Maggie sipped her coffee, then bit a Mexican vanilla truffle and rolled her eyes in ecstasy. "Bliss," she said. "So, what did you want to talk about?"

"Jeremy Mattox."

"I told you everything I know about him."

"Aw, come on, Maggie. You're interested in people, particularly young people. You probably know all his hopes, plans, and dreams."

"Those are pretty far from facts."

"I'll settle for surmises."

Maggie stared at the ceiling while she finished her truffle and took two more sips of coffee. When she finally spoke, she was frowning.

"Surmises are all I can come up with on Jeremy. He was pretty closemouthed about his hopes, plans, and dreams."

"So surmise."

"Jeremy never told me anything about himself. Where he was from, how he learned about the stage, why he was interested in the theater—I have no idea about any of that. If I try to describe him, he comes out sounding like a nonentity."

"A nonentity? Or a mystery man?"

"To me, a nonentity. To Jill, apparently a mystery man."

"You spent quite a while with her today. Did she tell you anything about him?"

"Very few facts. She did say he'd worked in Chicago theaters. Which made me wonder if he's working here under a fake ID."

"Why would he do that?"

"It's fairly common. To work backstage in a city like New York or Chicago, you have to belong to the union. The Warner Pier Showboat can't pay union wages or offer union benefits. So if a guy is desperate for a job, he takes it under a fake name."

"Would that be a reason for staging a disappearance?"

"I don't see why. If they get caught, they just drift away and deny the whole thing. The union isn't likely to track them down."

Maggie sipped her coffee and nibbled a treasure chest pastille. "Honestly, Lee, these kids face so many temptations! I worry, worry, worry about them. They think they're all grown up and know everything, and they don't know anything!"

Maggie shuddered. I remembered that at nineteen Maggie had gone to California to try to break into the movies. She has never confided just what happened, but I do know that there are episodes from that time that she deeply regrets.

"There are so many pitfalls," she said. "Bad guys are just lurking behind every potted plant, luring them into things that they'll be sorry for the rest of their lives."

"I know," I said. "Those guys hang around beauty pageants, too. The only thing that saved me from having nude photos on the Internet was my mom. If I was asked to go on a photo shoot, she insisted on going along. It's funny how fast a lot of photographers lost interest in me as a model."

Maggie laughed. "Did you ever have any interest in an entertainment career?"

"No! And a good thing, too, since I barely scraped by in the talent competition. I'd sing my medley of John Denver songs, smile, and retire to the back row, where the tall girls stood."

"But you got to the Miss Texas competition."

"One year out of the five I tried. I wasn't particularly disappointed. Accounting is a much safer way to make a living."

"Too bad you can't do an audit for the talent competition."

We both got the giggles at the thought of a beauty pageant that featured a contestant in a bikini with a ledger under her arm or wearing an evening gown and carrying a computer while demonstrating Quicken. It was a good five minutes before we got back to the subject at hand.

"Well," I said, "if you don't know anything about Jeremy, what have you figured out about Jill?"

Maggie frowned. "Lee, you usually avoid gossip. So I don't think these questions are idle curiosity. What are you up to?"

I quickly sketched my suspicion that Joe and I were intentionally being drawn into some plot. And I wasn't sure just what the plot was about.

"But why were we the first boat boarded?" I said. "And we were the smallest boat. All of the others have been yachts. After Jeremy disappeared, why did Jill run past five houses to ask us to help her? Why did this Hal—a friend of Jeremy's—want Joe to help him with a legal matter? And what's happened to Hal? After he asked Joe to meet him, why didn't he show up?"

"I see your concern," Maggie said. "But I have no idea what's going on."

"I'm sure you don't. But Jeremy and Jill seem to be part of it. Whatever it is. So I thought I'd try to find out more about them."

"Okay, okay." Maggie took the final bonbon, then stared at the ceiling before she spoke again. "You hit a nerve, that's all."

"With you? Why?"

"I guess I have a certain sympathy for Jill."

"Why?"

"Because I'm afraid she's headed for trouble, Lee."

Maggie leaned against the desk and looked at me with serious eyes. I could even see tears welling up.

"I worry about Jill, Lee, because she's just like I was at that age."

Chapter 10

My impulse was to go around the desk and give Maggie a big Texas hug. Then I remembered we were sitting in my fishbowl office, with all the world and Warner Pier able to look at us, so I restrained myself. I didn't want to call the attention of Warner Pier to the fact that Maggie had teared up.

I knew Maggie had many regrets about whatever had happened to her in California twelve or fifteen years earlier, but she had never confided the whole story to me. I also knew her real dread was that her husband, Ken, would find out all the details. If she had a good cry in my office—in full view of Fifth Street—the word was sure to get back to Ken, and he'd ask her about it.

Warner Pier is a small town.

So I shoved a box of Kleenex closer to her, and I tried to sound sympathetic. But I didn't give her a big hug.

"Maggie, you know you need to talk to some sort of counselor about this issue."

She nodded, but she didn't speak.

"I'll be happy to listen, just as a friend, any old time. But you need to put all that behind you, and I don't know how to help you do that."

She nodded again and blew her nose. "I'm sorry, Lee. Most of the time I handle it. But when I see somebody else headed over the same cliff I fell down, I tend to lose it."

"I hate to trot out the platitudes, but we all have to make our own mistakes."

"I sure made mine. But Jill is the same kind of girl I was at nineteen or twenty. She's ambitious. And she wants success now. Now! She's not willing to wait."

"And you think she'd be tempted to take a shortcut?"

"I'm afraid so. Especially since she's also absolutely fearless."

"Are you saying Jill might take a shortcut—seduce the director or something—if she had the chance? Or do you think specific shortcuts are being offered to her?"

"I don't know. Maybe I'm imagining things."

I sighed. "It's like we tell children: If you feel as if something's wrong, something probably is. You must have some evidence. What is it?"

"Oh, crazy phone calls. Stuff like that."

"Is Max involved? He's the director-producer. Do you think he might be in on some sleazy deal?"

"He hasn't shown any sign of it to me. Max doesn't seem to be the problem—he keeps his distance from the cast and crew. Spends most of his off time out in the community. I simply have an uneasy feeling about the situation at the Showboat. And I can't quite put my finger on why." Maggie leaned forward. "Anyway, no matter what's going on, I can't quit and leave 'em to it."

"Contract?"

"Right. I have to work through August thirtieth. So I just try not to notice the clique."

"Clique? As in small group of people who hang together?"

"That's right."

"So you think there's a small group of—is 'troublemakers' the right word?"

"'Conspirators' might be a better one. But I don't know what they're conspiring about."

"Maggie, anytime you have more than a half dozen people working together or studying together or whatever they're doing together—well, don't cliques of some sort develop?"

"Sure. But this is different. It's the stop-talking-when-a-nonmember-comes-in type of clique, not the let's-all-go-for-a-beer-and-not-invite-Maggie clique." She laughed. "I told you—it's probably my imagination. It's just a group of people you wouldn't think had anything in common, and they don't seem to socialize, but they all seem to have some secret link."

"Who's in this group?"

"Jill, Jeremy, and Mikki, mainly."

"But not Max Morgan?"

"No, he stays aloof from all of us. If that group is particularly close to him, I haven't noticed it. In fact, now and then he gives the cast and crew a little lecture on being one big happy family. I suspect he noticed the same thing I do and is trying to discourage it."

Maggie stuffed the final treasure chest into her mouth, chewed, and swallowed. "And now that I've gorged myself on TenHuis Chocolade, I'll repeat—probably I'm imagining the whole thing. And I'll get out of your office. And your hair. And if you mention one word of all this . . ."

I crossed my heart. "Hope to die," I said. "I will not break your confidence. Not even to Joe."

"Oh, Joe can be closemouthed," Maggie said. "I don't

know if I should ride it out or try to find out what's going on. Maybe I should talk to Max."

She left my office, waved at Aunt Nettie, and went out the front door, leaving me confused about just what to do next. Only one thing was certain. I wasn't giving up on trying to figure out why Jill had come running up Lake Shore Drive that morning, passing five other houses to reach Joe and me.

Then I looked at my watch. Five thirty. Yikes! My day off was nearly over, and I hadn't been to the grocery store yet.

Lots of couples splurge by going out on Saturday night. Joe and I were so busy all week that we splurged by staying home. It was the one night each week I made sure I produced an actual home-cooked meal. I jumped to my feet and headed for my van, trying frantically to think of something tasty but quick to cook.

Sounded like steaks. Maybe Joe would fire up the charcoal grill.

Two hours later we sat down to rib eyes, baked potatoes, and salad. Not too imaginative, but a treat. As we ate I told Joe about my visit to Camp Sail-Along and why I felt sorry for the camp manager, Jack McGrath, especially since he apparently knew nothing about sailboats. I left out the part about telling Jack that I might join him for a nap. Or a nip.

"You've had a busy afternoon, Lee."

"I'm determined to find out why Jill was so set on reporting Jeremy's so-called drowning to us. Which leads me to another question. Why did this Hal Weldon try to reach you?"

"Word of my superior legal skills had reached him, and he wanted to make a will."

"People rarely want to make a will so urgently that they call a lawyer on Saturday."

"My clients do. Poverty law, remember. The working poor usually can't afford to take off work during the week."

"Had you ever heard of Hal Weldon?"

"Not until the office paged me and said it was an emergency."

"So you don't really think it was a will or something else routine?"

"No, Lee. I think Hal Weldon is in some kind of trouble and needs a lawyer immediately."

"Has he been arrested?"

"Not in this county, as far as I've been able to find out."

"So you've been checking!"

"I asked Hogan, and I called the sheriff's office. Neither of them had ever heard of him. In fact, neither of them had arrested anybody today—Warner County not being a high crime area. I didn't try other counties."

"I wonder why he wanted you."

"I might have represented him in a previous life. Either his or mine."

"But you don't remember him?"

"Nope. I represented a lot of people in Detroit and more later in Chicago. I don't remember them all."

"Do you have a list of those old cases?"

"With names of clients? I'm afraid not. Since they were agency clients, I left their records behind."

"Besides," I said, "Weldon might be using a different name."

"Why do you say that?"

I told Joe about Maggie's idea that Jeremy might be working under a fake name to avoid union rules. "Since Hal Weldon was supposedly also a stagehand, I guess it's possible he would be using an alias, too."

Joe frowned. "Maybe Hogan could contact the stagehands union, find out something. The problem would be giving him an excuse to do that. As far as we can tell, no crime has been committed. Accidental drowning is of interest to law enforcement, true, but it's not illegal."

We finished eating in silence, and I got up and went to the kitchen for the ice cream I'd planned for dessert. But when I brought it back to the dining table, Joe was in the corner of the living room, looking at the computer screen.

I was surprised. "You don't want ice cream?"

"I'll be right there." But he didn't come. He kept sitting there, giving an occasional command to the computer.

"What are you looking for?" I said.

"I thought I'd find out if Hal Weldon has a criminal record."

"You can do that?"

"Within limits. Prison records are public. And they're online."

Before Joe's ice cream could melt, he'd discovered that Hal Weldon had never been in prison in Michigan or in Illinois.

Before he could hit the CLOSE button, I interrupted. "As long as you're looking, Google him. Maybe we'll find out something."

Joe shrugged, went to the Google site, and typed in "Harold Weldon."

"I'll put in Illinois, too," he said, "just so we don't get every Weldon in the United States." A moment later we both laughed. He'd pulled up fifteen hundred references.

"Better bring the ice cream in here," he said. "I'll try Hal Weldon. That might narrow it down."

It did. There were only fifty-some-odd references to Hal

Weldon that contained the word "Illinois" as well as his name. We learned that there are Hal Weldons who are doctors, Hal Weldons who appear in genealogical records, and one Hal Weldon who's a prominent steel guitar player.

And way at the bottom of the list, we found one that made me gasp, and Joe yell. "Bingo!"

"That's gotta be him," I said.

A Hal Weldon had been on the gymnastics team at South Chicago University three years earlier.

Joe and I both felt sure that we'd found the Hal Weldon who did "tricks" out behind the cottages at the Showboat dorm. But we hadn't found a picture of him. All we had was a listing of entries for intercollegiate gymnastics meets.

It was another lead. Joe cleared the table, and I loaded the dishwasher. Then we dug out our set of DVDs of classic comedies, watched one of our favorites, *Some Like It Hot*, and went to bed.

It had been a long day, and it was followed by an early morning. The phone rang at seven a.m.

The darn thing is on my side of the bed, so I picked it up. My hello was barely civil.

"Lee?" A deep basso resonated out of the receiver. "Max Morgan here. Sorry to call so early, but I wanted to catch you before breakfast."

"You did that." I groaned. Then I sat up. "Has Jeremy been found?"

"Not yet. But I want to talk to you."

"I go to work at noon. Come by the shop."

"I was going to invite you and Joe to go to brunch with me."

"Brunch?"

"At Herrera's. They open at ten. I need to talk to you both."

"What about?"

"I'll tell you there. Can you make it?"

I turned over and poked Joe. He opened an eye, and I repeated Max's invitation. He nodded. Or I think he did. I was awake by then, and I was getting curious about what Max Morgan had to say.

"We'll be there," I said.

"Good. I added up a few things about Jeremy, and I need your advice."

That got my attention. I climbed out of bed, made a pot of coffee, and headed for the shower.

Joe and I were looking spiffy when we walked into Herrera's at five after ten.

Herrera's is one of Warner Pier's more upscale restaurants. It features white tablecloths and a quiet atmosphere. I don't understand why most restaurants are designed to be noisy.

Herrera's overlooks the river, and it was another beautiful day. The French doors to the deck were open so that patrons could eat their omelets or eggs Benedicts outdoors. Max, however, had a table in a corner inside.

We were greeted by Joe's stepfather, Mike Herrera. He hugged me and patted Joe on the back, then led us to Max's table.

"I'll send a round of mimosas over," he said to Max, "just because you're entertaining my kids."

Max, Joe, and I all agreed that we never turned down mimosas, but Max looked worried, and the offer didn't make him look any happier.

"Let's order," he said. "Then I'll tell you what I found out. And you can advise me."

Talk about suspense. It was hard to make small talk until the waiter took our order and the mimosas came. Then we all leaned toward the center of the table.

"What have you discovered?" Joe said.

Max's frown grew deeper. "I think Jeremy may have rigged his own disappearance," he said. "Loan sharks seem to be after him."

Chapter 11

Loan sharks? I'd never heard of loan sharks in Warner Pier. We don't even have a payday loan office. That seemed like a strange idea.

Then I realized that Jeremy was in Warner Pier only for the summer. He lived most of the year in Chicago. And in Chicago, loan sharks could well be a major threat. Easy to get mixed up with, and hard to get unmixed from.

I was still analyzing Max's comment when Joe spoke. "Just why do you think loan sharks might be involved, Max?"

"Because of this strange guy who showed up at the theater last night. He was looking for Jeremy."

"Tell me about him," Joe said.

"He looked and acted like a tough guy. Hair slicked back. Deep widow's peak. Lips as thin as razor blades. Sneering mouth. Hard eyes. He was wearing a suit!" Max shook his head. "Talk about looking out of place in Warner Pier."

"Had you ever seen him before?"

"No. The guy just walked up to the box office last night. I was at the window, and I remember selling him a ticket, but I didn't pay much attention to him until after the play was over.

He stayed in his seat until about half the crowd had cleared. Then he tried to come backstage."

"Backstage?"

"Luckily I was able to head him off, so he didn't get a chance to bother any of the cast or crew."

"You're sure he was looking for Jeremy?"

"Yeah. I told him nobody was allowed backstage, and he told me he had business with Jeremy."

"Did he give you his name?"

Max shook his head.

"Tell me exactly what he said."

"I told him Jeremy wasn't there. He said Jeremy's name was in the program. I told him about Jeremy's accident, his disappearance. That's when he gave a big sneer."

"That was an odd reaction."

"I know. But that's what he did. Sneered. Then he growled in this raspy voice." Max dropped his own voice to imitate the man. "'Very likely.' That's all he said. But he said it as if he didn't believe me.

"I guess I got mad then. I told him the rescue team had looked for Jeremy all day, and that there were witnesses to his disappearance. Then he started quizzing me about who the witnesses were."

"I hope you referred him to Hogan," Joe said.

"I certainly didn't give him any names, and I told him where the police station is. But he said there was no need for the law to get mixed up in it. Then the guy said Jeremy owed him money. So I told him we were trying to locate Jeremy's next of kin, and it would be up to them to settle his debts."

"He said, 'They'd better.' God, Joe! His voice cut through me like a saw. A big, fat buzz saw. Like *Perils of Pauline*."

That comment mystified me; I couldn't keep from asking what he meant. "*Perils of Pauline*? What is that, Max?"

Max answered without looking at me. "It was a silent movie serial, nearly a hundred years ago. They used to tie the heroine to a log and threaten her with a buzz saw. The hero always arrived just in time."

Joe had been frowning. "The guy sounds like bad news, Max. Did you call the cops?"

"I threatened to do that. And he said, 'No need to get excited, pal.' Then he left. And I stood there and watched until I was sure he had driven away."

"What was he driving?"

Max shrugged. "Dark sedan of some kind. Big. I didn't get a good look. I was mainly concerned because I didn't want him bothering my cast and crew."

Our food arrived then, and I tried to settle down to a mushroom, cheese, and ham omelet while I listened to Joe and Max discuss the threatening stranger. I guess I succeeded at concentrating on their conversation; the next time I noticed what I was doing I'd cleaned my plate and downed a second mimosa.

Joe urged Max to call Hogan and tell him the whole story, even offering to go with him. Max said he would go alone. He promised to contact Hogan as soon as we finished eating.

It was after eleven when Joe and I said our thank-yous and got into my van. I was driving. Parking is always tight in downtown Warner Pier during the summer, even on Sunday mornings, so we had dropped Joe's truck at the boat shop.

After we'd gone a couple of blocks, Joe spoke. "What did you make of Max's description of the Chicago loan shark?"

"To be honest, Joe, he seemed to be describing a generic old-fashioned gangster. Thin lips, oily hair, spiffy suit."

Joe nodded. "I agree. Max's 'loan shark' may not have mentioned his name, but his appearance would be so unusual that I'd bet the Chicago antigang force could put a name to a guy who dressed like that."

"He would be distinctive today. Frankly, he sounded like the character George Raft played in the movie last night."

"Yeah. Except he didn't keep tossing a quarter."

"Neither did George Raft. That was a different character in the movie, a younger guy."

As I spoke I turned onto the short drive leading to Joe's shop. It was a typical sandy Michigan lane. A few loads of gravel had been spread on it once upon a time, but the gravel had been pounded down into the underlying sand, and snowplows had built low mounds of gravel and dirt on either side of the road, so the ruts were a rough combination of sand and gravel.

It wasn't a good road for a bicycle, but when I turned I saw one ahead of us.

It was ridden by a man wearing khaki shorts, a white T-shirt, and a black bike helmet.

I wasn't traveling very fast, but at the sight of the bicycle I slowed even more. The man moved over to his right. He hit the mound of gravel that edged the road. The bike's handle-bars seemed to go crazy, wobbling and shaking frantically.

Joe leaned forward. "Watch out!"

I brought the van to a dead stop.

The man looked over his shoulder, apparently checking on us, and his front wheel ran into a small branch lying on the edge of the drive. That wheel seemed to come to a complete halt, but the back wheel kept moving. The bike flew into the air, did a forward somersault, fell over sideways, and landed in the weeds beside the drive.

So did the rider.

It was like watching a stunt on television. The rider lifted off the seat and seemed to curl into a knot. He hit the ground in a fully tucked position, and he rolled along like a beach ball. His momentum whirled him over and over. It was quite gracefully done, but I expected the guy to be skinned from one end to the other.

Finally he stopped rolling and flopped onto his right side. That's when I saw blood on his knee.

Joe and I both jumped out of the van, calling out in unison, "Are you hurt?" Which was stupid, since we could see the blood running down his leg.

We ran toward him. By the time we got there, he had stretched his leg out, and he was pulling his bike helmet off. He looked familiar.

"I don't think it's serious," he said.

"Can you bend the knee?" Joe knelt to look at the damage.

The young man flexed the joint, then nodded. "Yes, it moves easily. I think I can stand up."

And he did that. I was surprised at how easily he seemed to manage getting to his feet. A similar roll in the gravel would have put me in the hospital.

When he was on his feet, I saw who he was, and I yelped at him. "You're the guy who saved the pirate ship!"

It was the nerdy-looking customer who had been in Ten-Huis Chocolade the afternoon Tracy nearly banged into the elaborate pirate ship displayed in our window. He was such an ordinary-looking person that I'd hardly remembered what he looked like. He was of average height. He had hair of an average brown, and shoulders of an average width. The only things striking about him were his buckteeth and his glasses. The glasses had a fashionable shape, but they held very thick lenses. Luckily, his dramatic roll hadn't broken them.

Joe led in questioning him. "Can you walk?" "Are you injured anyplace but the knee?" And finally, "Do you need an ambulance or a trip to the ER?"

"Oh, no!" The guy had an engaging grin, oversized teeth and all. "If I could borrow a chair so I could sit down and dig the gravel out of my knee . . ."

"Sure. We'll take you on to the shop in the van."

"Isn't that the shop?" We could see the building at the end of the drive, and he pointed at it. "I can walk that far. It'll loosen up my knee."

Joe walked to the shop with the bike rider, carrying the bike because one of its wheels didn't want to roll, and I moved the van down to the parking lot. I unlocked the door to the shop, went to the back room where Joe once had a tiny apartment, and dug out the first-aid supplies. I set out chairs in that back room—now it's basically a break room for Joe's boat business—and I let Joe take care of the injured knee. After all, in his days as a lifeguard Joe passed the first-aid course that particular job requires.

Luckily, Joe had a supply of peroxide, Neosporin, and Band-Aids. Within fifteen minutes our unexpected patient was bandaged up, and I was handing him an ice pack I'd created out of ice cubes that I'd retrieved from the miniature refrigerator and wrapped in a plastic sack and two clean shop rags.

"This is really nice of you," the young man said. "You shouldn't take so much trouble."

"If we hadn't startled you, you probably wouldn't have fallen," Joe said.

"If I wasn't riding a bike for the first time in seven or eight years, I wouldn't have lost control. It wasn't your fault at all. I'd better introduce myself. I'm Byron Wimp."

At least that's what I thought he said, and Joe apparently thought the same thing. We probably thought that because this guy looked like such a milquetoast that "wimp" was a word that described him. He was ordinary in size, shape, and appearance. If you added the thick glasses, the buckteeth, and the clumsy fall off his bike—well, he did seem like a wimp. But it was hard to believe that anybody was named "Wimp."

So Joe and I both repeated what we thought we'd heard. "Wimp?"

"Wendt. W-e-n-d-t. Byron Wendt."

Joe hid a grin. "Were you just out for a ride?"

"Yes, but it was a ride here. I heard that you have some great antique boats."

If Byron was interested in boats, I knew the conversation was going to get nautical. It was time for me to leave.

"I've got to get to work," I said. "Joe, can you take Byron wherever he needs to go?"

"Sure." Joe turned to Byron. "Do you want to look at the boats? Or go home and put your leg up?"

"I'd appreciate seeing the boats. And you don't need to take me back. I can call and ask my boss to come pick me up."

"Where are you working?" Joe said.

"Oxford Boats."

I had moved toward the doorway, but at that I swung around. "Oxford Boats? That means I have to ask you some questions."

Byron grinned. "You want to buy a yacht?"

"No. I'll stick with Joe's antique speedboats. But I work with two shifts of teenage girls, and if they find out I met someone who works at Oxford Boats and didn't ask about the Marco Spear rumor, they'll go on strike."

Byron frowned. "That's what the girls in the shop were talking about when the pirate ship nearly sank. Is the rumor still around?"

"Oh, yes. Is it true that he's buying a yacht from Oxford? And that he's coming to Warner Pier to pick it up?"

That got a toothy grin. "I haven't heard a thing about that. I'm a peon out there. All I do is clean toilets—I mean heads— and sweep upholstery. The boss wouldn't tell me about his celebrity clients."

"There aren't any rumors going around the yard?"

"I've been there just a few weeks, so I might not have heard them. But I have noticed that the owners kowtow to their clients." His voice was slightly derisive. "The customer is definitely always right at Oxford Boats. So if Marco Spear is coming to pick up a yacht—and they've got a honey waiting for somebody—they won't let the word get out to the riffraff who work in the yard."

Joe and I smiled at his comment. I told the two of them good-bye and turned toward the door again. I was still within listening distance when Byron Wendt spoke to Joe.

"I guess we have a common acquaintance. You must have known Jeremy Mattox, the guy who drowned yesterday."

I couldn't resist stopping to hear what came next. Why on earth would Byron Wendt think we knew Jeremy? Did we have some connection with Jeremy—something neither of us knew about? I had to know.

All Joe said was, "Why do you think Lee and I knew Jeremy Mattox?"

Byron Wendt's eyes blinked rapidly.

"He specifically mentioned you in the message he sent me through my mother—I thought you must know him."

Chapter 12

Silence followed that announcement. I'm sure Joe was as astonished by it as I was, but I was the first to speak.

"I'm calling the shop to tell them I'll be late. I'm not leaving until I understand all this."

Joe shook his head, looking mystified, and turned toward the refrigerator. "Let me get you a soda, Byron. We need to hear the whole story."

He got out canned pop for Byron and himself. I found a chair for Byron to use to prop his leg up. Then we questioned the guy.

"First," Joe said, "who *is* your mother? Do we know her?"

It turned out that Byron's mom was a Mrs. Wendt who lived in New Jersey and who had merely passed Jeremy's message along. Apparently she had nothing to do with Warner Pier, Jeremy's disappearance, or the dead man at Beech Tree beach. No, we didn't know her.

"I guess Jeremy called her because he didn't have a number for me," Byron said. "I went to high school with Jeremy, and he came over to my house a few times, so he knew how to find my mom. But Jeremy and I have been out of touch for three or four years."

Byron said he had been surprised when his mom said Jeremy had called. And the message Jeremy left made no sense to him.

"Something dangerous is going on," Jeremy had told Mrs. Wendt. "Byron needs to know about it. If I don't get hold of him, tell him I'll leave a message with Joe Woodyard. He's a lawyer there in Warner Pier."

"So Jeremy knew you were in Warner Pier?"

"Yes. But I don't know how he found that out."

"Did your mother give him your number?"

"No." Byron blinked behind his thick lenses and spoke wistfully. "I guess you'd say I've sort of moved on from the old gang. It's not that I don't want to talk to them, but sometimes they ask questions I can't answer."

Yeah, I thought. Questions such as, Why are you working as a gofer at a boatyard after the other members of that old gang finished college and are now trying to build careers? I could understand why Byron might not want to speak to his old friends.

"Anyway," Byron said, "Mom told him that she'd pass the message along and ask me to call him. He left a number, but when I called it, no one answered. I sloughed the whole thing off, but then I heard on the television that Jeremy was missing and that some other guy was dead. So I thought maybe I'd better—you know—do something about it. But I don't know anything the cops would want to know, and Jeremy had told my mom that you could explain . . ."

"You were pretty calm about being told you were in danger."

"I didn't believe it. I still don't."

"You're not a threat to anyone?"

Byron shook his head.

"Do you have anything valuable anyone would want to take?"

"No way!" Byron's eyes got wide, and his gaze was direct. "Right at the moment, my bike is the most important thing I have, and it now needs a few repairs."

"Did the call scare your mother?"

"I think she felt the same way I did. Jeremy was always overdramatic. Neither of us took it seriously."

"Did you know Jeremy was in Warner Pier for the summer?"

"I sure didn't, and I don't know how he found out I was here. My arrival got very little attention."

"This is a small town. Maybe he saw you on the street."

"I didn't see him. Besides, I've only been here a few weeks, and I've been hanging around the boatyard. I've only been downtown a few times." He smiled at me. "You know, for chocolate. The people at the boatyard ate the box you gave me, so I had to go buy more."

"I'm glad you liked it."

"I do. And the girls are always—you know, pleasant."

I hoped Byron hadn't tried to date any of the girls. Then they might not have been so pleasant. I was sure they'd have said no. He certainly wasn't love's young dream.

Joe wrote down the phone number Jeremy had left with Byron's mother, then thought the whole thing over a few minutes before he spoke again. "Byron, could I talk to your mom directly?"

Byron thought. "Sure. It's Sunday. She ought to be home. Maybe her story will make more sense to someone else."

He produced a cell phone from his pocket and called the number for us. After his mom answered, he explained why he had called and said Joe wanted a firsthand account of Jeremy's call. Then he put the phone on the speaker setting so all three of us could follow the conversation.

Not that it turned out to be much of a conversation. The only thing notable was that Mrs. Wendt had a nasal Jersey accent. That struck me as odd, because her son's accent wasn't so pronounced. Okay, okay—I minored in speech, and I think regional accents are interesting, though they're disappearing fast, largely because of the influence of television. So I notice the way people talk.

But whatever her accent, Mrs. Wendt didn't have a lot to add to the story Byron had already told us.

"Jeremy said a dangerous situation had arisen," she said. "He said Byron needed to know about it. And he said that he'd explain it all to you, and Byron could call you if he wasn't able to reach him. Reach Jeremy, I mean. Did Jeremy tell you what's going on?"

"No," Joe said. "As far as I know he didn't even try to call me."

"Maybe the whole thing is a hoax," she said.

"What would be Jeremy's purpose in starting such a hoax?"

"That I don't know. But why did he call me, anyway? Calling a mother to tell her that her son may be in a dangerous situation—and then not describing the situation—well, I admit that I hope it was a hoax."

Byron spoke then. "I thought it was a hoax. Or a joke of some kind. I was going to just ignore the call until I heard that Jeremy had disappeared."

Joe asked Mrs. Wendt exactly when Jeremy had called. The call had come in two days earlier, about ten o'clock in the evening, she told us. "I told him it was kinda late."

"Huh." Joe grunted, then sat silently, apparently thinking over what she had said.

So I took the opportunity to ask a question.

"Mrs. Wendt, were there any sounds in the background when Jeremy made his call?"

"Sounds?"

"Dogs barking. Horns honking. Ice cream trucks tinkling."

"None of those things." She laughed. "I did get a snatch of Elvis."

Joe, Byron, and I all spoke in unison. "Elvis?"

"Yeah. It was some recording of an Elvis Presley song. 'You ain't nothin' but a hound dog.' I heard it for just a minute. It wasn't loud. Then the sound went dead. At the time I thought Jeremy had hung up. But maybe he put his hand over the speaker. Or maybe it was a radio or some other phone cutting in."

"And you didn't hear the sound again?"

"No, just that few seconds of 'Hound Dog.' Elvis complaining that he was crying all the time. Or some other part of the lyric."

That seemed to cover the subject. Joe took Mrs. Wendt's number, asking her to call him if Jeremy phoned her again. He gave her his cell number. Then all four of us said goodbye. And I left for the office. I couldn't put off going in any longer.

The place was crowded when I arrived. Instead of going to

my office, I joined Tracy and Brenda behind the counter, boxing up bonbons, truffles, and molded chocolates as quickly as possible. I'm always surprised at the way tourists buy our chocolate. After all, a chocolate fanatic could buy a half dozen Cadbury Caramello bars—that happens to be my own favorite mass-market chocolate bar—for about what he or she would spend for a quarter of a pound of TenHuis Dutch caramel bonbons. Yes, our bonbons are better, but superficially the product description is the same for either product: "creamy, European-style caramel filling coated in dark chocolate." Well, maybe the Caramello is coated in milk chocolate.

After about twenty minutes, the three of us had caught up with the rush, and I was able to talk to the girls a few minutes.

"How was the movie?"

They looked at each other, but neither answered.

"Yesterday," I said. "I ran into Will, Brenda, and he said you all were going into Holland to a movie. What did you see?"

"We didn't go," Brenda said. "We changed our minds."

Tracy couldn't stand it any longer. She blurted out what she knew. "They stayed home and had a big fight!"

"Oh, gee!" I said. "I'm sorry to hear that. Fights are never fun."

I looked closely at Brenda. She didn't seem distraught. In fact, her mouth had a grim appearance that looked more angry than upset.

Throughout the summer's troubles with Will, I'd tried hard to keep from telling Brenda what to do about them. I tried to keep from even hinting at how she should handle her problems with Will. For one thing, I'm not her mother. For another, telling kids how to handle their romances sensibly is almost certain to cause them to do the opposite of what you suggest—in other words, to handle them stupidly. It's a no-win situation, and I wanted to stay out of it.

So I didn't say anything else. Instead, I went into my office and sat at my desk. To my surprise Brenda followed me, closing the door behind her. So she apparently wanted to talk to me.

When she spoke, she kept her voice low, and I concluded that she still hadn't confided in Tracy. "It's this Marco Spear thing again. Will keeps nagging me about it."

"I'm sorry to hear that!"

"I'm getting really tired of it." She leaned over my desk and spoke firmly. "And I'm not planning to marry someone who can't take a joke. No matter how sexy he is."

She gave a firm nod, straightened up, and went back into the retail shop.

So there.

She still hadn't asked my advice. Good.

I tried to do my own work, but I couldn't help keeping an eye on Tracy. My dad, a small-town Texas mechanic, would have said she was "about to bust a gut." She was so curious about what Brenda had told me that she could hardly keep from jumping up and down and screaming.

Twice she made some excuse to come into the office and talk to me about nothing. When she spoke to Brenda, she was obviously trying to pretend nothing was wrong. I concluded that she had quizzed Brenda earlier and had been refused information. Tracy didn't act angry; after all, she couldn't admit to being mad at Brenda for refusing to share her personal business.

At least Tracy's reaction was funny. I wasn't surprised

when she came into my office a third time. I looked up as she came in, wondering what her excuse was now. To my surprise Tracy offered me an envelope.

"I'm sorry," she said. "This fell out of the door when we opened up at twelve. I forgot all about it."

At first I thought she was handing me a piece of trash. It was a preprinted envelope, a little bigger than six inches by three inches. It had probably come from some publication. It was the sort of envelope, usually begging me to subscribe, that annoys me by falling out when I try to read a magazine.

Not only was it a common, usually useless, item, but it was also dirty. It was smudged with actual dirt, plus someone had scribbled all over the front of it with a marking pen.

In other words, it looked like a piece of trash. I'm sure I frowned at the sight.

"I nearly threw it out," Tracy said. "Luckily, I looked at the back."

I flipped the envelope over. It was sealed. And written across the flap was "Please deliver to Joe Woodyard."

There was no name, street address, or box number for the sender, and the envelope had not been stamped.

When I looked at the front, I saw that the scribbling there wasn't purposeless. The original address had been crossed out, and the word "Over" had been scrawled across the bottom.

"This was stuck into the door?" I probably sounded as puzzled as I felt.

"Right. Brenda and I thought it was kind of peculiar."

"I think you're right."

Tracy's tone was eager. "Are you going to open it?"

"It's addressed to Joe. I'll take it to him."

"It sure is weird." Tracy went back to work.

"Weird" did seem to be the word for it. A hand-delivered message was unusual enough. And the makeshift envelope—that was strange, too. And for it to be delivered to my office, not to Joe's and not to our home—well, that was unexpected.

It was beyond weird. It was mysterious.

My mind immediately jumped to Hal and Jeremy—the two missing guys. And Hal had wanted to meet with Joe on a legal matter. Could this note be from Hal?

Heaven knows how I resisted the temptation to rip that envelope open.

Instead I picked up the telephone and called the boat shop.

Joe, darn him, wasn't there. So I called his cell phone. It was turned off.

Where could Joe be?

I reviewed the day's activities. We'd had brunch with Max Morgan, then talked with Byron Wendt about Jeremy.

Joe might think both conversations should be discussed with Hogan Jones.

I called the police station.

The phone was answered by the county dispatcher. It was Sunday, so all calls to the Warner Pier PD were being handled by the Warner County Sheriff's Office, thirty miles away.

I apologized for bothering the dispatcher and hung up. But I wasn't giving up. Next I tried Hogan's cell phone.

And I nearly fell out of my chair when Joe answered it.

"Joe? I thought I called Hogan."

"He's busy. When he saw your number, he handed me the phone. What's up?"

"You got a strange message. In writing. Delivered to Ten-Huis Chocolade."

"That is odd. Who's it from?"

"There's no return address." I picked the envelope up and examined it again while I described it to Joe.

He answered with a noncommittal grunt.

I was more curious than ever. "Where are you and Hogan?"

"At the police station."

"That's just a couple of blocks. I could bring the envelope over."

"No. Hogan doesn't need any callers this afternoon."

"What's going on?"

Joe lowered his voice. "You know that body we pulled out of the lake yesterday?"

"The drowned man? I'm not likely to forget it."

"It turns out he wasn't drowned."

"Wasn't drowned!"

"Nope. The preliminary autopsy found a bullet hole hidden in all that dark hair."

Chocolate Chat
Gardeners Like Chocolate Plants

Cacao isn't the only "chocolate" plant. Some gardeners grow flowers and vegetables that are "chocolate."

These don't taste like cocoa; the term describes their color. Most of them are that dark, rich brown verging on burgundy that we call chocolate.

The Cherokee Chocolate tomato, for example, is a dark red with a deeper, almost brown color near the stem. The plants are touted in magazines as producing tomatoes weighing from ten ounces to a pound.

Other "chocolate" plants include a cosmos, a sunflower, a viola, and the chocolate pincushion flower.

Near Langley, Washington, on Whidbey Island, is the Chocolate Flower Farm. The farm is actually a nursery specializing in dark-colored flowers, especially chocolate ones.

Chapter 13

I gasped. "Oh, no! Does Hogan know any more details?"

"Not yet. He just now found out about it."

"Have they figured out who the guy is?"

"No."

I had a million other questions. Had anyone been reported missing who might be the dead man? Were any of the marinas missing a boat? Were any swimmers missing? My questions came pouring out.

"Hang on!" Joe said. "Hogan is doing everything possible to find out about the guy, but it takes time. Somebody's got to miss him before anyone knows he's gone. It's only been two days."

"Could he have shot himself?"

"Not in the back of the head."

"Oooh. Yuck."

"I'm nearly through here at the police station. I brought Byron by to make sure he reported that phone call from Jeremy. When we got here Hogan had just heard the word about the guy in the lake being a shooting victim. I'll leave in a few minutes and take Byron back to the boatyard—or wherever he needs to go. Then I'll come over to your place to pick up that message."

"You're sure you don't want me to bring it over? It might be from Jeremy, if he isn't dead. Or from Hal, if he isn't dead either."

Joe sighed. "I started to ask you to read it to me, but it might be a privileged communication. I'll be there as soon as I can."

It was thirty minutes before Joe arrived, and if I had thought Tracy was going to bust a gut with curiosity about Brenda—well, I was definitely leading in the gut-busting contest during those thirty minutes. I was dying to know what was in that envelope. I longed to rip into it. It didn't do any good to tell myself it was probably something like a bill or a receipt or a note asking Joe to serve on a committee. I couldn't think of any reason that a bill or a receipt or an ordinary note would have been delivered to TenHuis Chocolade on a Sunday, rather than to the Vintage Boats post office box on a Monday morning. But why would a message to Joe from anybody at all come to TenHuis in the first place? And why in a makeshift envelope?

I was chewing my nails by the time Joe got there. Of course he could tell how curious I was, so he teased me. He dawdled around before he opened the odd note, looking at both sides of the envelope, holding it up to the light, pretending to sniff it, then acting as if he was going to slip it into his pocket unopened.

Finally I brandished my letter opener at him. It's shaped like a miniature sword, and I held it up like a dagger. "In a mystery novel," I said, "this would be a great murder weapon."

Joe laughed. "Give me the letter opener—handle first, please."

He slit the top of the envelope carefully, then spread the top open, turned it over, and made a motion as if he were emptying the contents. Nothing came out.

"No mysterious white powder," he said.

Finally, Joe reached inside the envelope and pulled out a small sheet of lined paper. It had a ragged edge, as if it had been ripped from a notebook. He read it. Then he shook his head, rolled his eyes, and tossed the message over to me.

As I read it, he called out, "Tracy! Did you do this?"

"What? What have I done now?" Tracy came running into the office.

I held up the small sheet of paper, and she read it aloud.

"'If Marco Spear comes to Warner Pier, he'll be in danger!'"

Tracy's eyes bugged. "Who would threaten Marco Spear?"

Joe shook his head. "I don't think anyone would, Tracy."

"But this message . . ."

"Is a fake," he said. "Some kind of publicity stunt, maybe. Silliness."

"What does it have to do with me? Did you think I would write something like that?"

I answered her. "We don't really think that, Tracy. Joe just means it probably came from someone who knows how interested you and the other counter girls have been in the rumor about Marco Spear. Whoever wrote it was teasing you."

"But then why was it addressed to Joe?"

"I don't know. Joe? What do you think?"

"I have no idea. All I know is that someone has been trying to link us to the pirates all along, and now they've started on the top pirate, Marco Spear. I'm tired of it."

"Do you think we should show it to Hogan?" I said.

"Hogan has a dead man on his hands. I don't want to bother him with a silly note."

Joe swore Tracy and Brenda to secrecy, asking them not to mention the note. "Let's not start any new rumors," he said.

Both agreed to keep the note quiet, especially because Joe said he was sure it was a joke of some sort and that the two of them might be intended targets of the joker. Joe and I both knew that asking for a direct promise was the best way to keep Tracy from talking. We'd sworn her to secrecy in the past, and she'd always kept her word. Brenda wasn't quite as talkative. Or maybe, being a summer worker only, she didn't know as many people to talk to. But it was good to make her promise not to talk about it, too.

I had been a bit surprised, however, that Joe showed the two girls the note at all, but he explained quietly that he thought satisfying their curiosity about it might keep them from talking. I hoped he was right.

Joe left, saying he was going to go back to the boat shop to try to do some work. "Varnishing a hull sounds real soothing right now," he said. "I want to forget this whole business."

I noticed that he took the odd note with him, although he left the envelope behind.

I wasn't quite ready to forget the matter. I looked the envelope over. "Business Reply Mail." The words were printed in big letters and enclosed in a rectangular box. Underneath that box, in smaller letters, it said, "Postage will be paid by addressee." I had seen thousands of envelopes like it. Whenever I pick up a magazine, it seems that a half dozen of them fall out.

The address—the street address of the business that promised to pay the postage—had been obliterated with a heavy black marking pen, apparently the same pen that had been used to write Joe's name. When I held the envelope up to my desk lamp, I couldn't read the address.

The flap was quite deep—two-thirds of the depth of the envelope—and had been thoroughly glued down. I took out my scissors and carefully cut it just above the line of glue. I got most of the flap up.

That didn't help much. The words "Yes, I want to subscribe to" were at the top, but the magazine's name had been blacked out with that darn black marker. I held the envelope up to the light again. I could take a guess at the second word that had been blacked out, and I thought it was "today."

The first word, however, could be anything. "Chocolate Today." "Boatbuilding Today." "Teaching Today." I squinted at the first word. It did start with *T*, I decided.

Could it be "Theater"?

Could the envelope have come from a theatrical magazine?

My heart skipped a beat at the thought that I might have discovered a real clue, but I told myself not to get too excited. Even if the word was "theater," it wouldn't prove anything. Practically everybody we'd run into over Jeremy's disappearance and the dead man found at our beach had some connection with theater. Besides, an advertising envelope like that one—if it was designed to encourage new subscriptions to a theatrical magazine—might be in any magazine for the artistically inclined. A literary magazine. An art magazine. A dance magazine. *Theater Today* might try for subscriptions in dozens of different publications.

I carefully put the envelope in a file folder and was tucking it into my top drawer just as the phone rang.

"TenHuis Chocolade. Fine chocolates in the European tradition."

"It's Joe, and don't say my name."

"Okay." I paused. "What's up?"

"Can you come over to the police station?"

"Yep."

"Quick as you can, okay?"

The girls were too busy with customers to ask questions, so I muttered something about needing to do an errand, and I left. I did tuck the file folder with the envelope in it under my arm.

At the police station I found Joe in Hogan's office. The two of them looked a bit worried.

Hogan didn't even say hello. He opened with, "Lee, I need your help."

"Anything I can do, Hogan."

"I need to talk to Jill Campbell again. She's at the theater, and I don't want to pick her up in a patrol car. It would cause too much talk. I thought maybe you could arrange to bring her to meet me."

"She may not want to go anywhere with me, Hogan. We didn't part on very good terms."

"You should make it plain that I'm the one who wants to talk to her. If she refuses a polite request, then I'll make an impolite one. But I'd like to try it this way first."

"I'll call Jill and tell her I'll pick her up. Where do we go?"

"Here. Your van is parked in this block enough that no one will think anything about it."

I glanced at my watch. "The current Showboat production has a matinee this afternoon. Jill might not be able to get away until after the performance."

Hogan grimaced. "Then I'll have to wait. I need to be

friendly with the citizens of Warner Pier, and sabotaging the Showboat is no way to accomplish that."

He stood up. "In the meantime, I'll go out to Oxford Boats to talk to Charles Oxford. I'll try to find out whether there's anything to this Marco Spear rumor."

I gestured toward Joe. "I gather you two are a bit more concerned about that threatening note than Joe indicated."

Hogan rolled his eyes. "It sounds like a bunch of kids calling in a bomb threat so they can get out of school for the day. Just silly. If it's not . . ."

"You don't dare ignore it."

"Right. But I don't want to feed the rumor mill."

"Before you go," I said, "I found out a little more about that message." I opened my file folder and showed the envelope to Joe and Hogan. They didn't seem too impressed with my reasoning, but Hogan put the folder away carefully before he left.

I checked my watch. "The Showboat performance doesn't begin for fifteen minutes," I said. "Maybe I can catch Jill now." I picked up Hogan's phone and called the theater box office. It took a while, but someone did call Jill to the phone. I explained what Hogan wanted.

Jill's answer sounded petulant. "Why does he want to talk to me? I've told him everything I can."

"He didn't explain to me, Jill. He just asked me to phone you because he thought you'd prefer not to be called to the phone by the chief of police or hauled into the police station in a patrol car. I can pick you up."

"Okay, okay! I'll meet you at the stage door as soon as the performance is over. That should be shortly after five o'clock."

I hung up. "Okay, Hogan's chore is done. I guess I'd better get back to the office, though I'm not getting much done today."

"Could you do me a favor first?" Joe said. "Call Maggie for me. Didn't you say she isn't working in this week's Showboat production?"

"No, Maggie's not onstage this afternoon. But why do you want me to call her? You can do it yourself."

"Not and sound sort of casual and gossipy. I think you'd get better results than I would."

"Results on what?"

"I need to know more about this Hal who tried to set up an appointment with me."

"Maggie's not real happy about being regarded as a source of information about the Showboat cast and crew."

"I know. But you can tell her Hal tried to contact me, and I'm afraid he's in trouble."

"That's the truth."

"It sure is. And I need more information about him."

Luckily, Maggie was home. I decided to be blunt. "Maggie, Joe wanted me to ask you for some information about a potential client."

I put the phone on speaker, so Maggie's answer reverberated. "Tell Joe I'm not touting for business for him."

Joe laughed. "Believe me, Maggie, our little poverty-law office has plenty of business. This guy made an appointment with me here in Warner Pier, then didn't show up for it. I'm wondering if he's in hot water. He was formerly connected with the Showboat, so I thought you might know something about him."

"Who is it?"

"His name is Harold Weldon. He goes by Hal. He was on the technical crew at the Showboat early in the summer."

"Oh!" I could hear the relief in Maggie's voice. "He left before I joined the company."

Maggie explained that she'd shepherded several of her students through a speech competition just after school was out. "So I joined late. I remember people mentioning this Hal, but I never saw him."

I gasped as the implications of her statement hit. "Oh, Maggie! If you never saw him, he might be the guy at the beach!"

Then a second thought popped into my mind. "That won't work. Jill saw him, too."

"Jill didn't look at his face. Besides . . ." Maggie paused. "You know, I think Jill joined the company the same week I did. She might not have known him either."

Joe made a sort of growl deep in his throat, got up, and went into the outer office.

I kept talking to Maggie but quickly learned that she'd not only never met Hal; she'd not heard much about him either.

"Sorry I bothered you," I said. "At least we learned something." We hung up.

When I followed Joe, he'd already called Hogan. "I hated telling him that one of his ID eliminations was based on faulty information," he said. "He was sure the guy on the beach wasn't Hal because Maggie had seen him. And now we find out Maggie didn't know Hal."

"Yeah, but if a person who did know Hal will take a look at the body . . ."

"Right. Even if the dead man isn't Hal, Hogan will be further ahead."

I went back to the office. Brenda and Tracy had managed fine without me, and we closed up promptly at five. I drove over to the Showboat to pick Jill up. I managed to time my arrival pretty well. A parking place opened up just as I drove by.

This was like a miracle, because the Showboat's parking lot is small. And, no, it's not because the Showboat is surrounded by water. It has water on only one side. The Showboat, despite its name, isn't a boat at all. It began life as a warehouse.

The Showboat Theater is up the Warner River, a half mile or so inland from downtown Warner Pier. Way back in 1890-whatever, the structure that houses the Showboat Theater was built as a warehouse where peaches, apples, grapes, blueberries, and other Michigan fruits were packed and shipped. It was on the waterfront so that the fruit boats could sidle up to the warehouse's dock and the fruits could be loaded on board easily.

After fruit began to be shipped by truck more often than by boat, the building became derelict. In the 1980s an entrepreneur installed a stage and seating to make it into a theater holding around 125. Two years ago, when Max Morgan took over its operation, a deck was added on the side nearest the water. This allowed members of the audience to buy a drink at the lobby bar, take it outside, and look at the river between acts. Some theatergoers also came to performances in boats and tied up along the deck.

But all entrances to the theater were on the land side. The audience went in at the west end, and the cast and crew at the east. So after I parked my car, I took up my station at the east end.

The day had been another Lake Michigan prizewinner—temperature in the seventies, humidity in the twenties, no breeze, sun shining. It was pleasant standing there waiting, nodding to people as they came out. Then someone called my name. "Ms. Woodyard? Nice to see you."

I turned to face a dark-haired girl nearly as tall as I am. "Remember me?" she said. "Mikki White."

Jill's roommate, the girl who got her tongue tangled the way I do. I greeted her.

"Jill's nearly ready." Mikki leaned close. "She said she had to fix her makeup before she could face more questions."

So Jill had told Mikki that Hogan wanted to talk to her. So much for keeping the session quiet as a favor to Jill.

"Can I ask you something? Is it true you did some beauty pagans?"

What in the world was she talking about? It took me a minute to figure out that she was talking about pageants, not pagans.

"Well, Mikki, the first thing you have to learn about them is to call them 'scholarship pageants,'" I said. "I took part in five of them. Made it to Miss Texas competition once."

"Did it help your career?"

"No. Being a loser in the Miss Texas competition is not a big help in the chocolate business. My mother pushed me into pageants because she thought it might make me more poised."

"Did it?"

"Maybe."

I continued to talk to Mikki, discussing the pros and cons of pageant participation. It was fifteen or twenty minutes before I realized that Jill had never come out of the theater.

Chapter 14

Mikki, displaying great innocence, agreed to help me look for Jill.

She took me backstage and showed me all around. We saw the dressing rooms, the prop storage, the wardrobe room, and the stage. Mikki called out Jill's name as we toured, but of course Jill didn't answer. And, also of course, Mikki swore she didn't have any idea where Jill might have gone or how she got out of the theater without my seeing her.

I refrained from slapping Mikki into next week.

I didn't even say anything angry, although irate words flitted through my mind. Jill had flown. But taking my annoyance out on Mikki—her accomplice—wouldn't accomplish anything.

I left and went to the police station, where Hogan was waiting, and told him what had happened. He didn't seem too upset, or even too surprised.

"I tried to be a good guy," he said. "So Jill's got only herself to blame if she now has to deal with me as a bad guy."

I kept thinking about Maggie and her fear that Jill was willing to cut corners because of her ambitions. But I'd promised

Maggie that I wouldn't say anything about that. So my reply had to be oblique.

"What's worrying me is that Jill may be dealing with a *real* bad guy," I said. "After all, someone's been killed."

"That's one of the things that worries me, too. I'll go by her room over at the Riverside, but I doubt Jill's there, and I'm not sure where else to look for her since I'm not getting any cooperation from her or her friends."

"Have you found any of the theater people who can try to identify the dead man?"

"Max Morgan said he'd do it first thing in the morning."

Hogan and I sat silently; then I spoke. "Did you find out anything at Oxford Boats?"

Hogan's gaze dodged away from mine. "Nothing very helpful."

I interpreted this to mean that he'd found out something but he didn't want to share it with me. I went home.

Joe was already there, and his greeting gave me a broad hint that Hogan had found something out.

"Let's take the boat out," he said.

"Do we have time before dark?"

"Grab some crackers and cheese. We can go out to dinner after we get home."

There's no reason, of course, not to take the Shepherd Sedan out on the river or lake after dark. It has all the proper lights and equipment. But Joe and I like to look at the scenery when we go out on the water, so we usually go before sunset.

This evening Joe was in a hurry. He stood at the back door jingling his keys while I grabbed a box of Wheat Thins. By the time I'd stuck a couple of cans of Diet Coke in a small cooler and put on a sweatshirt, he was already waiting in the truck. He started the motor as I locked the back door to the house, and he pulled out of the drive before I could buckle my seat belt.

"What's up?" I said.

"I just want to get the boat down the river before it's too much closer to sunset."

Maybe so, but I was suspicious.

Joe's boat shop is on the Warner River, and he's lucky enough to have a small dock. In the summer he leaves the Shepherd Sedan tied up there. He whipped its cover off and had the motor going before I could untie the mooring lines. Once I was in the boat, he took off. He couldn't go too fast on the river, where no-wake rules apply, but he didn't dawdle.

This obviously wasn't a casual cruise, but I decided not to ask any questions. For one thing, it's hard to talk over the gurgle-gurgle of the Shepherd's motor. That gurgling sound is one of the main attractions for fans of antique powerboats, but it means the boat has to be anchored if you're going to carry on much of a conversation. It's still not as loud as most modern boats.

I settled back, listened to the gurgle, and watched the trees on the bank go by. We'd be out on the big lake in time to see the sunset. Whatever Joe was up to, it was a nice way to spend a summer evening.

We proceeded down the Warner River, passing the mansions and summer cottages that line its banks. Then the river widened, and we came to the harbor. The houses and businesses of Warner Pier were now on both sides of the water. We went under the bridge that linked the two parts of the town. This was a busy area, with plenty of boats coming and going, and Joe slowed even more. We saw lots of people we knew.

We inched past more than a mile of marinas and saw Maggie and Ken McNutt strolling past the boats and eating ice cream. We chugged past Herrera's deck—filled with diners. My longtime friend Lindy Herrera—now Joe's stepsister-in-law—was on duty, supervising the restaurant for her father-in-law, and waved at us. We passed the park that borders the river. Then came more quaint cottages and dozens of beautiful summer homes.

I was beginning to look for Warner Point, once a showplace estate and now a city conference facility, when Joe suddenly pointed ahead. I could hear his yell of delight over the motor's gurgling.

"There it is!"

Ahead of us was the gorgeous new yacht that had been constructed at Oxford Boats. We'd all seen it under the huge boat shed, a hundred yards or more from the river, but that had been an indistinct view. Now it was out on the water, where we could get a closer look.

Joe cut the motor back to idle, and as the noise level dropped, I spoke. "That's what you're up to! You heard that the new yacht was going to have a test run tonight."

Joe grinned. "Hogan got a strong hint and passed it along."

"It's beautiful!"

The Warner River is about a hundred feet wide at that point, and the yacht was so big that its stern seemed to fill the channel. Actually, it filled only about a quarter of the channel, but the yacht was a whole lot bigger than any other boat on the river that evening.

Its name was painted across the stern—*THE BUCCANEER*. I pointed that out to Joe. "That just about proves it really is being purchased by Marco Spear," I said.

The craft was shiny and white, with chrome accents here and there. The upper deck swept back like a spaceship. Its design was as sleek and elegant as a cigarette boat's—only it was four times longer and three times wider than those snazzy speedboats are. It could have been used as a set for a science fiction movie.

"Golly!" I said. "It looks as if it might take off for Mars."

Joe gave an appreciative moan. "You're right. You know how neat it looks when the lake is real calm, and the reflection of the moon makes a path? I believe this baby could follow that path right into the sky."

"I wonder how big it is."

"It's a hundred and sixteen feet long, with a beam of twenty-four feet. It sleeps a dozen and takes a crew of six."

"How do you know all that?"

"I looked it up on the Oxford Boats Web site. It's a version of their model XZ200. Here—you take the controls so I can get a good look at it."

We switched places, and Joe picked up his binoculars and went to the tiny deck at the back of the Shepherd. From there he could look over the top of the roof that covered our seating. I kept the sedan headed down the channel, moving slowly. We weren't gaining on the yacht. This was lucky; late on a Sunday evening, the river was crowded. Boats were coming toward us, ready to tie up at their docks and at the Warner Pier marinas. And since everybody on board those boats was gawking at the yacht just the way Joe and I were, a collision would have been pretty easy. I kept my eye on the traffic, ready to throttle back if I needed to, and tried not to stare only at the yacht.

"Where do you think they're going?" I said.

"Out on the lake to open her up."

"Do you want to follow her out?"

"I'd love to get a view of something besides her stern."

Joe took the wheel again, and we followed the gorgeous yacht as the channel narrowed. Still moving at no-wake speed, the big boat went by the rock walls that mark the entrance to Lake Michigan, past the Warner River's own little lighthouse, and out into the swells of the big lake.

The Shepherd Sedan began to pitch and roll. I knew my stomach wouldn't stand too much of the lake.

"They'll speed up now," Joe said.

But the yacht kept moving slowly until it was a few hundred yards offshore. Then it turned so that its side was toward the land, which meant it was also toward us and the other dozen small boats that were hovering there trying to get a look at the yacht.

"She's posing for us!" I said.

I had the binoculars now, but I didn't need them to see that the bigger boat was rolling in the waves the same way the Shepherd Sedan was.

"Why are they staying there, with the waves hitting them broadside?" I said. "If they'd head into the waves at an angle, it wouldn't be as rough. Or am I wrong?"

"No, you're right. Of course, they have a stabilization system. But even so . . . Here, you take the wheel, if you don't mind. I'll look it over; then you can have a turn."

I held the wheel—the Shepherd steers like an automobile—while Joe stood up on the deck again. Then he came back to the helm and took over. "Your turn," he said.

I crawled out from under the Shepherd's roof and stood up, hanging on to the roof and to my stomach. Propping my elbows on the roof, I looked the yacht over. There seemed to be about a dozen people on board. And one of them was look-ing directly at us and waving like mad.

"It's Byron Wendt! He's waving to us!"

Joe laughed. "I thought that was him. I guess a few peons got to go on the test run."

As we watched, the big yacht turned toward the sunset again, its prow pointed into the waves. Now we were again looking at its stern. Byron climbed up a companionway and joined a group on the flying bridge.

Suddenly the yacht's motor's roared. It began moving away from us.

A huge wake came up behind it.

"Sit down!" Joe yelled. He leaned forward to close the front windows. "We're going to buck like one of your Texas broncos!"

I slid into the closest seat. I could see the froth and dis-turbed water of the yacht's wake rushing toward us. In sec-onds the Shepherd was bouncing around like a fisherman's bobber, dancing across the water while waves five feet high washed over our bow. If Joe hadn't closed the front windows earlier, he would have had a wet lap.

It took several minutes for the wake to stop shaking us around, and those minutes nearly did me in. I hung on to the back of my seat and to the seat in front of me. And to my stom-ach. I hadn't eaten since that morning's brunch, or I think I would have lost everything down to my toenails. Poor Joe. He loves fooling around in boats, and he married a woman who gets seasick anytime the waves are more than a foot high.

Actually, the waves don't bother me. What bothers me is the drop into the space between the waves. Joe has given me the nickname "Wyatt." As in Earp.

He turned around and grinned. "I think you've seen enough of the fancy yacht, Wyatt."

"My stomach has."

He was right. I'd had enough of rising up, swooping down, and sliding sideways in a small boat on a large body of water. Lots of times Lake Michigan is calm enough to keep my stomach quiet. That wasn't one of the times.

"Hand me the Wheat Thins," I said. Something salty helps me fight motion sickness.

I stayed where I was, ate a handful of crackers, and opened a Diet Coke while Joe took the Shepherd back through the channel into the Warner River. There, at no-wake speed and on the calmer water, I moved up to sit beside him. He patted my hand. "Sorry about that. The lake was pretty choppy tonight. And I didn't anticipate that they'd take off so suddenly."

"That yacht was quite a sight. If Byron got to make the first trip, he must be more important out at Oxford Boats than he admitted."

"I think Byron is somebody's nephew."

"He sure was closemouthed about whatever's going on out there."

"He probably doesn't know much. And now, how about dinner at Herrera's?"

"Brunch and dinner both at Warner Pier's best restaurant? I think I could handle that."

"First, I'd better stop for gas."

We stopped by the Warner Pier Marina, where Brenda's boyfriend—or was he?—Will VanKlompen came out to fill the Shepherd's tank.

We took time to talk to Will, of course. He asked whether we'd seen the new yacht, where we were headed—all the polite questions. Then Will moved close to Joe. "My propeller shaft is leaking. Have you got a wrench that would tighten it up?"

"Sure. You need to borrow it?"

Will launched into a technical explanation of what he needed to do to the old boat he was always working on, and Joe said that he had a wrench that would handle the job.

"You can pick it up tomorrow, Will."

"I can't do that. I have to work an extra shift. I'll be here from six a.m. to nine p.m."

"It'll have to be Thursday, then. I have to go to Holland Tuesday and Wednesday."

Working at a job with regular hours was putting a serious crimp in Joe's boatbuilding career. But Will agreed to call him and set up a time when he could go by the shop to borrow the wrench, even if it had to be as far away as Thursday.

Brenda's name was not mentioned, though she'd mentioned Will's that afternoon. I knew they had a date after Will got off duty at the marina at nine o'clock, if the fight they'd had hadn't sabotaged it.

I vowed once again not to get involved in Brenda's romantic life, and Joe and I puttered on up the river to Herrera's. We tied up at the outdoor deck, went inside, and had a delicious dinner, complete with wine and candlelight. By then my motion sickness had passed completely, and I was hungry enough to eat my way through the whole menu, item by item. I restrained myself to salad and one entree.

We made the final leg of our trip, back up the river to Joe's boat shop, by moonlight. It had been a wonderful evening.

We had been ready for a wonderful evening. The past few days had not been wonderful. The search for the drowning victim, the runaround from Jill Campbell, the mysterious appointment with Hal that didn't happen—all these things had been puzzling, and we'd felt that we were required to deal with them on our own, because they were simply puzzling. Until the autopsy discovered that the man found in the water had been shot, they hadn't seemed to involve any crime, so we hadn't turned to Hogan.

In some weird way, learning that the man found dead at our beach was a murder victim had lifted a load from my shoulders. It was awful, of course. But I didn't have to do anything about it. Now it was the responsibility of Hogan Jones and of the Michigan State Police.

As we went up the Warner River, our motor gurgling, I was content. The moon was full and making a path across the water. We'd treated the inside of the boat with mosquito repellent, so nothing was chewing us. We were wearing snuggly sweatshirts. And we were together. Content. That's the word.

By then Joe was using not only running lights, but also a spotlight, which he played along the banks of the river. When the spotlight hit his dock, he cut the boat's speed. We sidled up to the dock, and I moved to the stern and picked up a short oar Joe keeps in the boat, mainly to shove the sedan away from the dock when it seems as if it's going to bump it too hard. The mooring line was coiled at my feet. I was still standing there when Joe spoke. His voice was urgent.

"Back off, Lee! Don't tie up yet!"

Huh? I swung toward Joe.

He was facing the controls. The motor revved, and I saw Joe throw the gearshift into reverse. The boat began to back away from the dock.

Then feet pounded on the little dock, and a dark figure ran toward me.

"Get down!" This time Joe yelled.

I guess I was too surprised to react. I didn't get down; I kept standing in the stern.

There were only four or five feet of water between the boat and the dock when the dark figure jumped toward me.

In an awkward imitation of a football block, I threw out my arms and stiff-armed the jumper while he was still in midair.

The figure landed in the water with a mighty splash, and I fell over backward just as a shot was fired.

Chapter 15

The next impression I had was of darkness.

"Lee!" There was a big thump from the front of the boat. "Lee!"

"Joe!"

"Don't move!"

"Joe! I'm okay! What happened to the lights?"

"I'll get us out of here. Stay down!"

Joe didn't have time to explain, but by then I had realized that he had killed all the Shepherd's lights. I wondered vaguely why there was no light coming from the shop, where Joe has a big outdoor light that illuminates the whole area. It wasn't on.

But that wasn't a major worry at the moment. I managed to get to my knees on the boat's deck. Then I heard splashing, and suddenly the side of the boat dipped, sinking toward the dock.

I yelled, "He's trying to climb in!" It wouldn't be hard for the guy who had jumped off the dock to get into the boat, since the river was only about four feet deep where he had gone in. All he had to do was stand on the riverbed and swing a leg over the side.

Joe yelled again. "Stay down!"

My hand met the short paddle. I grabbed it and got to my feet.

"I'll hit him!" I swung the paddle. I was hoping for the guy's arm or leg, but the thunk of wood hitting wood told me I'd hit the gunwale instead.

"I'm behind you!" Joe was moving toward me. I was afraid I'd hit him instead of the man who was trying to climb into the boat, so I didn't swing the paddle again. I stayed still, afraid to move a muscle, for a moment. Then the boat tipped again. The attacker was still trying to climb into the boat. I had to stop him.

"Watch out! I'm going to hit him again!" I said. I felt along the gunwale.

And my hand met strange fingers.

I shrieked. The hand grasped mine. I grasped his. We clung together in a sort of mad handshake.

The situation turned to total confusion. I still had the paddle in my other hand, and I began to whack at the attacker's fingers with it. He hung on, twisting my hand painfully. I couldn't get a good swing with one hand, so my whacking wasn't very effective. If I'd had a hatchet I could have done some real damage. Probably to myself.

Joe wasn't beside me. I figured that out when the Shepherd's motor began to chug, and the boat moved. In the dark I didn't know what direction it was moving.

The guy in the water still had hold of my hand, and half the blows I was aiming at him were hitting my own knuckles. Finally I dropped the oar on the deck, leaned over, and bit the guy on the wrist. He cursed and turned my hand loose. Then he gurgled, apparently because he had lost his footing and his head had sunk below the surface of the water. But the boat was still tipping toward him, so I knew he had kept his grip on the gunwale.

During all this, still in complete darkness, Joe had been falling over seats, kicking soft drink cans around, and generally raising a ruckus. He and I were both yelling out stupid remarks. "Get him!" "Start the boat!" "I can't see anything."

Then the motor stopped its gentle chugging and gunned hard.

The moment that happened, the guy hanging on the side let go. Once he wasn't pulling the side down, the Shepherd bounced up, and I nearly fell over backward again. By then my eyes had grown accustomed to the dark—we were under trees, so the moon was no help—and I had a vague sense that someone was climbing onto our dock.

I yelled, "He's getting away!"

Then I saw lights far away. They were bouncing off the trees that arched over Joe's drive.

I tried to yell louder than the motor. "Someone's coming!"

There was motion on the shore. A running figure—two figures—crossed between us and the bouncing lights. The lights grew brighter. A vehicle turned into the parking area beside Joe's shop.

Joe cut the motor to idle, and we both yelled, "It's Will!"

Will drives an old Jeep SUV. I had recognized the way his headlights are set and those aggressive vertical bars Jeep puts on its front ends, and I guess Joe did, too. That front end has pulled into our drive a lot of times.

Now Joe and I began our confused yelling act again. "Go back!" "Stay in the car!" "Drive off!" "Go away!"

I didn't know who had tried to waylay us at the dock,

but I did know someone had fired at least one shot. I had a horrible vision of Will and Brenda innocently stepping out of Will's car and meeting the bad guys with guns face-to-face.

Our shouting, naturally, produced exactly the opposite effect from the one we'd wanted. Will turned the Jeep around so that its headlights were shining on the dock, then drove a dozen feet or so closer to the river. He and Brenda got out and ran toward us, giving their own confused yells. "What's wrong?" "Where are you?" "What's happened?"

Joe gave a sigh. "I guess the bad guys have gone," he said. "Whoever they were."

He turned the boat's lights back on and used the spotlight to scan the bank. Then we came into the dock again. This time Will caught our mooring line and secured it to the cleat.

He and Brenda were full of questions, but Joe urged us all to get inside the shop before we began to talk.

"And lock the door," he said.

I had a horrid feeling that the intruders would be waiting inside, but the door was still locked, and when we got inside the shop, everything seemed undisturbed. Once we'd called the cops and I'd tested the plumbing, we all began to try to figure out what we'd seen, making notes so we could pass them along to the lawmen.

Brenda and Will hadn't seen anything.

"We were sitting on the deck at the Dockster having a soda," Will said. "We saw you guys go by, headed upriver. And I thought we could meet you at the shop and I could borrow that wrench tonight. When we got here, we didn't see any vehicles parked in the drive or on the road leading in. Joe's truck was the only vehicle. The first we knew that something was wrong was when we pulled into the parking area here. All of a sudden you guys began to yell."

"Joe?" I said. "What made you know something was wrong? You told me not to tie up before I saw a thing."

"The light outside the shop was out."

"Oh. I didn't notice that until later. The spot on the sedan is so bright, I didn't even realize that the shop light wasn't on until you doused the boat's lights."

"The shop light could simply have burned out, so that might not have meant anything. I think maybe I saw movement, too. Anyway, the situation just looked funny. I'm not entirely sure why."

When Hogan came—seems as if the poor guy is always coming to help Joe and me out after some emergency—we repeated our story.

"What I don't understand," I said, "is why? What was the point of all this? Were they trying to rob us? That's stupid. Nobody carries a lot of money or valuables when they go out on a boat. If they wanted the boat itself—which is worth quite a bit of money but would be hard to sell—it would have been easier to wait until we tied it up and went off and left it alone."

Joe spoke quietly. "You're forgetting the shot."

"At this point, Joe, I'm not positive that I heard a shot. In fact, it doesn't make sense. If the guys—and I'm sure there were two of them—had a pistol, why didn't they use it again?"

"That's a good question, Lee. And my question is, why are you alive?"

"Me?"

"Yes. I had a good view as the first guy ran onto the dock. He did have a pistol."

Joe reached over and took my hand. "I yelled when I saw him."

"You yelled for me to get down."

"Right. The reason I yelled was that he was standing squarely on the dock and aiming that pistol right at you."

"All I saw was the figure. I didn't see the pistol."

"It was there. He aimed right at you and fired from no more than five feet away."

He squeezed my hand. "I still don't see how he could have missed. By all rights, you should be dead."

He blinked, and I saw tears in his eyes.

I got a few tears in my eyes to match. Neither of us could say much, and Brenda, Will, and Hogan got a demonstration of effective mutual hugging. It must have been nearly five minutes before I could get another word out.

"Okay," I said finally. "We're back to the question we've had all along. Why?"

Hogan nodded. "A lot of strange things have happened, and you two seem to be concerned with them. But I sure don't see the reason. Lee, you're positive that you'd never seen the dead man before?"

"I swear. He was a complete stranger."

"Joe?"

Joe grimaced. "I can't swear, Hogan. I've represented a lot of people. And people's appearances change. I don't remember him, but I can't say he's not a former client."

Hogan nodded. "We'll see what happens in the morning, when Max Morgan takes a look at him."

Joe and I stayed in our own house that night, but I don't think either of us slept much. Anyway, I was at the office a half hour early, and not just because I knew Aunt Nettie was going to have lots of questions. If I'm just lying in bed staring at the ceiling, I figure I might as well get up.

Joe left even earlier than I did, saying he wanted to see what was going on at the shop. Hogan had left a patrol car overnight and had promised that the state police would have a crime-scene crew there early the next morning.

"Maybe they'll find a bullet," Joe said.

"Do you think it hit the boat?"

"I hope not!" Joe and I both chuckled. We both know his boats are just slightly behind me in his affections.

"Don't you think it went into the water?" I said.

"Probably. If that's what happened, even a metal detector might have trouble finding it in the weeds and mud."

At ten o'clock I was comforting myself with a cup of coffee and my substitute for pancakes, a maple truffle ("a round milk chocolate truffle flavored with Michigan maple syrup"). I jumped when the phone rang.

"Hi," Hogan said. "I've got a picture I want you to take a look at. Can you come over?"

"Be right there."

I walked the two blocks to the police station as quickly as possible. When I got there, somehow I wasn't surprised to see Joe pulling into a parking place. We walked in together.

Hogan didn't say anything. He simply motioned us back to his office and pointed to the computer screen.

"Can either of you pick out Hal Weldon?"

"I've never seen Hal Weldon," I said.

"Take a guess."

The black-and-white photo displayed was a group shot of a gymnastics team. It was even labeled "South Chicago Gymnastics Team," along with a date five years earlier.

I sat down in Hogan's chair, and Joe leaned over my shoulder. We spoke at the same time.

"Dark-haired guy," Joe said. "Back row."

"Second from the left. Tallest one there," I said.

I looked at Hogan. "And I'd definitely say he's now the late Hal Weldon."

Hogan nodded. "So you both identify him as the dead man. That's what I thought, too. The name in the caption is 'Harold Weldon.' But did you ever see him alive?"

I shook my head no immediately, but Joe hesitated.

"He does seem familiar," he said. "His hair was shorter when that picture was taken."

Joe went into the outer office, and in a minute I heard him talking on his phone. "Minnie? How're you doing?"

I knew Minnie was the office manager at the poverty-law office where Joe had worked in Chicago. So apparently Joe wanted to check on some case he'd handled then. That would have been at least five years earlier, or about the time the gymnastics team had posed for its photo.

Having picked the dead man out of the group, I began to look at the rest of the team members. Immediately one almost screamed, "Me!" It was one of the people in the middle row. This fellow had medium brown hair, lighter than Hal Weldon's, and he wasn't as tall as Hall. But his sleeveless gymnastics outfit displayed particularly broad and powerful shoulders.

I punched PRINT. Hogan said, "I'll get it," and I realized the police department printer was in the outer office. In less than a minute I was looking at a hard copy of the photo, only a bit more murky than the one on the screen.

The guy looked familiar, but I couldn't remember where I'd seen him.

I looked at Hogan. "Where's the cutline on this photo?"

"It's a separate file." Hogan picked up a printout from his desk. "Here's my copy. You might want to read the front row."

The third person in the front row was identified as Jeremy Matlock.

"Matlock? That's awfully close to Mattox," I said. "I guess Jeremy really was working under an alias. Max may have brought him to my office, but I wouldn't recognize him from this picture."

"And we still don't know where Jeremy is—whether he's Mattox or Matlock. We don't know whether he's dead or alive."

Hogan and I hadn't had time to say anything more when Joe popped his head in through the doorway.

"I defended Harold Weldon in a malicious mischief case," he said.

Chapter 16

"Minnie's going to fax some records of the case over to Mom's office," Joe said.

"We have a fax machine here," Hogan said with a grin.

Joe grinned in return. "Yeah, but I need to look the case over before I tell you about it. There's that darn confidentiality rule I've got to follow. But maybe the stuff Minnie sends will remind me of what it was about."

Joe and I had stood up to leave when the outer door swung open so hard that it bounced, and Max Morgan made an entrance. The theater director was wearing an all-black outfit—black jeans, black dress shirt, and black tennies, but he'd added a silk scarf striped in jewel tones and draped inside his collar as an ascot.

As soon as he was inside, he stopped and struck an attitude, holding his left hand in the air dramatically.

"Alas! Poor Yorick. I knew him, Horatio. A fellow of infinite jest."

Joe gave a cough that I recognized as smothering a laugh—not that laughing would have been out of place, since Max was obviously joking.

Hogan spoke mildly. "Graveyard antics, Max?"

Still being dramatic, Max stepped forward. "Forgive me, Hogan. I'm nervous, and it makes me clown. I'm here to take a look at your dead man. Not my favorite way to spend a morning."

I remembered then that Max had agreed to look at the body found on Beech Tree beach. But he'd agreed to do that when we hadn't known who the dark-haired man was. Now Joe and I had identified him from his photo.

Was further identification necessary? I opened my mouth to ask, then shut it without saying anything. If Hogan thought Max didn't need to look at the body, he wouldn't have him do it.

Joe and I said our good-byes without further comment. Joe headed for his mom's office, and I went back to mine. An hour and a half later I was working away on our fall sales brochure when Hogan called.

"It's official," he said. "Max ID'd the dead guy as Hal Weldon."

I looked toward our retail shop and gave a gasp.

"Am I supposed to act surprised about the identification?" I said. "If I am, tell me quick. Max is coming in our front door right now."

"There's no secret about the ID. Let me know what Max has to say. But don't forget that the cause of death is just between you, me, and Joe. I'm not announcing that before I have to." Hogan hung up.

Max waved the counter girls away and walked straight into my office. "Lee! Lee! What an experience."

"You need chocolate, Max. A few flavonols will settle your nerves. And I'll get you some coffee from the break room."

Max was persuaded to accept a raspberry cream bonbon ("red raspberry puree in a white chocolate cream interior, with an exterior of dark chocolate") while I got coffee for both of us. He sat down in the chair I keep for visitors.

"That was not a happy experience," he said.

"Hogan says you were able to identify the man."

"Oh, yes. His name was Hal Weldon. He worked as a stagehand for a week or two. That was early in the summer. He quit suddenly, leaving me with quite a hole to fill."

"Why did he quit?"

"He said he got another job, one that offered room and board."

"He didn't tell you where this job was?"

"No. I hadn't seen him around Warner Pier, so I assumed he'd left town."

I asked a few more questions, such as whether Max had any information on Hal Weldon's family, but he didn't seem to know any more. I began to wonder why Max had come to see me, unless he simply wanted a free chocolate.

Finally Max leaned forward with an air of getting down to business.

"Lee, I'm worried about Jill."

"Jill? I don't think I can help you there, Max. She and I bumped heads, you know."

"No, I didn't know."

"Yes, I asked a few pointed questions about just why she and Jeremy went swimming at Beech Tree Public Access Area so early in the morning, and she didn't seem to like my attitude."

"Why shouldn't they go there early in the morning?"

"The beach doesn't get any sun until after eleven."

Max blinked. "Oh."

"She was supposed to meet me after the matinee yesterday, and she didn't show up. Why are you worried about her?"

"I still think Jeremy disappeared deliberately. I'm sure he didn't drown."

"And?"

"I'm afraid Jill helped him."

I considered that. "I doubt it, Max. She was quite distraught over his—disappearance."

"I know she was, but I'm still worried. I think she's hiding something."

"What makes you think that?"

"Whispering. Strange phone calls. Evasive answers. A general atmosphere of secrecy."

"That's not necessarily because of Jeremy. Girls have lots of secrets."

"True." Max shook his head sorrowfully. "I'm not in loco parentis, not responsible for these students who work at the theater. But—"

He broke off, and I chuckled humorlessly. "Believe me, I understand. I supervise our counter girls, and one of them is my stepsister."

"It's just—" Max broke off again, looked around as if he were making sure the counter girls hadn't crept up behind him, then lowered his voice slightly. "I'm afraid I saw Jill with that strange guy I suspected was a loan shark."

"The guy in the suit?"

"Yes. But now I wonder if I understood the situation properly. His dealings with Jeremy may not have involved high-interest loans."

"Then what?"

A frown crossed Max's face. "Drugs? Who knows? I just didn't like him. An unsavory type."

I considered this. It didn't jibe with the impression that Jill had made on me. She hadn't seemed to be the type of person who might get involved with drugs. And while Maggie had expressed concern about Jill, along with other young and ambitious actors, she hadn't mentioned drugs. Surely ambitious young actors knew that drugs could ruin their careers before they were started. Acting takes discipline, and drugs destroy discipline. That's not hard to grasp.

Before I could tell Max that whatever was bothering Jill, I didn't think it was drugs, he stood up. "I guess I'd better get over to the theater," he said. "My cast and crew are there now striking the set, and I ought to be acting interested."

"You don't have a production this week, do you?"

"We're dark until Friday, when we open *Pirates*. Which means we rehearse all week."

As soon as Max was out the door, I called Hogan, as he had requested, and reported on our conversation. Did I feel like a spy? Yes. But I couldn't refuse Hogan. He'd simply done too much for me.

Then I called Joe's mom's office, hoping that Joe was still there. His mom's assistant told me he'd left an hour earlier, as soon as his faxed material arrived. So I tried the boat shop. Joe was there and seemed pleased at the idea of my bringing him lunch.

I ordered sandwiches from the Sidewalk Café, so it was nearly one p.m. when I pulled into the boat shop's parking lot.

I admit that revisiting the scene of the excitement we'd had the previous evening was scary. I looked behind every bush as I drove down the drive and into the lot. If there had been wind, if the bushes and trees had been moving around, I doubt I would have had the nerve to get out of the van. But this was Michigan, not Texas. It wasn't windy. It was a mild and sunny summer day. Still, I parked and looked the area over carefully. I saw nothing but Joe's truck. I got out of my van, and I forced myself to walk slowly into the shop.

No boogeymen jumped out at me. No guns fired.

After what Joe had said about client confidentiality, I was determined not to ask him about the case in which Hal Weldon had been involved. I didn't want him to tell me that he couldn't say anything about it. So I didn't say anything more inquisitive than "Here's your roast beef with horseradish sauce on a hoagie roll."

I might have burst with curiosity if Joe hadn't handed me the faxed sheets as soon as we sat down to eat.

I read the first page, then began to laugh. "Joe! This is that case about the college guys who crashed the St. Patrick's Day parade!"

He smiled. "The funniest case I ever handled. Nice to know one of the guys involved thought I did a good enough job that he wanted to hire me again. I hope that isn't the reason he wound up dead."

"I doubt that his decision to contact you had anything to do with his death."

"Hard to tell."

I kept reading the faxed sheets. As Joe said, the case had been amusing, and the dry legalese of the papers Minnie had sent didn't hide that.

The case had involved a half dozen college students, all

athletes at South Chicago U. The mascot of South Chicago just happens to be the Viking, and that probably had some relationship to what happened.

The six guys, apparently at an all-night beer party on the eve of St. Patrick's Day, had decided that the Irish were over-emphasizing leprechauns, shamrocks, and the Blarney Stone and were not giving enough credit to the Viking side of their heritage. After all, the beer drinkers figured, the Norsemen had raided the Irish coast regularly. One of the students even claimed that Vikings founded the city of Dublin.

About four in the morning and after a couple of cases of beer, it became clear to the group that it was their responsibility to change the emphasis of the upcoming St. Patrick's Day parade in downtown Chicago to help the event reveal this to the public.

One of them borrowed a flatbed truck from his father's business—without permission—and two others turned some scrap lumber into a makeshift ship's prow, complete with cardboard dragon head. A sail made from a bedsheet was hoisted. Some girlfriends came up with fake fur garments. At a school with a Viking mascot, horned helmets were readily available in the band room and were pressed into unauthorized use.

The resulting mishmash, put together in about six hours, must have looked as if it had been raided by Vikings.

The group then joined the parade—without paying an entry fee or getting permission. They simply cut into line somehow and participated for eight or ten blocks before the parade authorities and some of Chicago's finest yanked them out.

Joe got involved because, after they sobered up, none of them could afford a lawyer. He represented them in police court on the day after St. Pat's.

"I will say I never saw a more repentant group of criminals, or at least a group with such a mass hangover," he said when he got to that part of the story. "Especially when they had to face the irate Irish parade organizers."

"The Irish were upset, were they?"

"A bit. Of course, you have to remember that their heads probably ached as much as the Vikings' heads did. They were all but yelling, 'String 'em up!'"

"How'd you get the college guys off?"

"I didn't entirely. But it was a matter of convincing the parade people that they were going to give the Vikings even more publicity if the case came to trial."

"And they were going to look even more stupid."

"I let their own lawyer explain that to them. Or maybe their parade chair did it. Anyway, the six Vikings pleaded guilty to disturbing the peace and got off with fines and a strong scolding from a judge whose name happened to be O'Brien. I remember he warned them to stay away from the Sons of Italy. Those guys get even more incensed about Vikings."

"Because of Leif Erickson?"

"Oh, yes. They don't like to be told that he came over before Columbus."

I swallowed a bite of my ham sandwich. "So Hal Weldon was one of the Viking Six. Was he one of the leaders of the prank?"

"I'd guess that he was more of a follower. Anyway, I think all six of them lost their athletic scholarships."

"Too bad!"

"Yeah, I hate to see that sort of initiative punished."

"I guess there's no way to find out why Hal made an appointment with you."

"There's the tattoo clue."

"The skull and crossbones on his arm?"

"Right. That's a pretty good indication that he was one of the Warner Pier pirates."

I bit off another mouthful and chewed it while I considered that. "But why would the Warner Pier pirates need a lawyer? As far as we know, they haven't committed any crime."

"That's what worries me."

"You mean they haven't committed a crime—yet?"

Joe nodded. "Neither Hogan nor I can figure out what they're up to. Which makes us suspect that it hasn't happened yet."

I couldn't figure it out either, of course, and I needed to get back to the office. I was clearing away our luncheon debris when I heard a voice outside.

"Ahoy! Ahoy, the shop!"

Joe looked as mystified as I felt as he opened the shop's door.

The figure outside was so ordinary and nerdy looking I could barely remember his name. Luckily, Joe did.

"Hi, Byron," he said. "I see you're back on your bike."

"Yes, and I come bearing an apology."

"Apology for what?"

"An apology for nearly swamping your boat when the new yacht was on her test run last night."

"Apology accepted. We shouldn't have gotten so close. And you weren't at the helm."

"True. I've also got an invitation."

"An invitation?"

"An invitation to be on board her when Mr. Oxford takes her out for another test run tonight."

Chocolate Chat
Chocolate May Help Fight Malaria

The Gates Foundation, the organization founded by Bill and Melinda Gates to fund philanthropy, education, and research, has given a $100,000 grant to a young scientist to study using chocolate to combat malaria.

Steven Maranz, a researcher at Weill Cornell Medical College, received the grant through the foundation's Grand Challenges Exploration program. The program funds research that's considered somewhat outside the box, but Maranz's project, although unusual, is based on conventional science.

Instead of killing the mosquitoes that carry the malaria parasite, Maranz is investigating interrupting their life cycles. The parasite exists on fat. Chocolate bonds with cholesterol and takes that fat out of circulation. Theoretically, this could starve the parasite.

Maranz hopes to kill most of the parasites but leave enough to give children a lifetime resistance to malaria. He plans to administer the "medicine" in a form similar to hot chocolate. Chocolate bars, he says, won't do the trick.

Chapter 17

Joe has this fabulous smile.

When Byron Wendt told him he could have a ride on the new yacht, that smile broke out like the sun coming out after a Lake Michigan thunderstorm. It just spread all over the place and chased every dark cloud away.

Even when he frowns, Joe is definitely the best-looking guy in west Michigan, but when he cuts loose with that smile— well, I practically have to sit on my hands to keep from grabbing him. Sometimes, naturally, I don't bother to sit on my hands, but I didn't want to shock Byron Wendt by jumping on my husband right in front of him.

So I gulped and spoke to Byron. "How come you're the one who gets to hand out the invites?"

"Another part of my errand-boy duties," Byron said. "Is this an acceptance?"

Joe yelled his answer in true Michigan style. "You betcha!"

Byron told us to be at the front gate of Oxford Boats at seven p.m., and we assured him we would be.

Joe was still smiling. "How'd we get on the list?"

"Mr. Oxford invited a few of the local boat people." Byron grinned almost as broadly as Joe. "I even got to invite a couple on my own. So I picked Tracy and Brenda."

"Oh, gee!" I said. "They'll think they died and went to heaven. But why'd you pick them?"

"They've been nice to me."

Byron pedaled off then, and I tossed out the lunch debris. "Joe," I said, "just why do you want to go on this boat ride?"

"Boat ride? That's a pretty mundane term for an excursion on one of the most technically advanced and beautifully designed new yachts constructed anywhere in the world this year. This yacht is Arab-oil-magnate stuff."

"I know. And I guess that's why I want to go along. I'd just like a look at the way the other half lives. But you're a real boat person. You look at it more professionally. Would you like to own a yacht like that?"

"If I did, I would have stuck with the Chicago firm. I could have bought a yacht and moored it at a marina there, then lived on it. Used it like an apartment." Joe laughed. "Of course, the problem with that would have been that I would have had to work so hard to support my yacht that I'd never have had time to take it out on the water."

"That kind of a yacht is pretty different from the boats you own and work on here."

"I love my wooden boats best, Lee. But maybe it's like an architect who specializes in affordable housing going to visit a cathedral. It's interesting to look at it even if he's never going to build one."

"The wooden boats aren't exactly affordable. They cost the earth."

"True." Joe came around the table and took me in his arms.

"Don't worry. I'm not going to start lusting after a yacht. I'm happy with the Shepherd." He nuzzled my ear. "As long as you go out in it with me."

I drove back to the office feeling content once again. I love it when Joe looks happy. When we first began to see each other, he didn't look happy very often. Life had given him some hard knocks, and he had to be tough to deal with them. In those days, he usually tended to look deadpan, which was the expression he used to hide angry or frustrated feelings.

Now he frequently looked happy, and I was conceited enough to think I was part of the reason.

My life was also a lot happier with Joe in it. Yes, I was a contented woman. I put aside all thoughts of pirates and drownings and strange people who waited in ambush at Joe's dock. I had a job I loved; I had a man I loved; I lived in a town I loved. I had friends; my bills were paid; I had clothes on my back, food on the table, gas in my van. If I'd been walking, I'd have skipped.

I even thought happily of how excited Brenda and Tracy must be to have an invitation to go out on the fancy new yacht—one that might even belong to Marco! Marco! Marco!

I was laughing as I drove down our alley and parked in my reserved space. I did give that little skip—probably looking like a giraffe stumbling—as I opened the back door of Ten-Huis Chocolade and went into our break room.

As soon as I was inside, I heard Brenda. She was yelling. "You're just jealous!"

Brenda and Will were facing each other in the middle of the break room, nose to nose—or they would have been nose to nose if Will hadn't been so much taller than Brenda. His blond head was ducked toward her dark one. She had thrown her own head back and was meeting his stare angrily. Both of them had their fists on their hips. Their body language told it all; a serious fight was going on.

Brenda's voice was loud. "And you have no reason to be jealous!"

"Oh, no? I've spent the whole summer listening to you rave about that movie star!" Will's sneering tone turned "movie star" into an insult.

"Marco? He won't be there! It's just a boat!"

Will's answer was sarcastic. "Oh, but you'll get to see all the places he will be. The gym where he'll work out. The kitchen where the hired help will give him a snack. The main salon, where the big-screen TV will play his movies! The bedroom—"

"Don't get insulting!"

"Come on, Brenda! You don't need to go on that yacht!"

"You'd go! You'd go in a minute!"

"I wouldn't go without you!"

That stopped the discussion. Mainly because it was an obvious lie. Everybody in Warner Pier was dying to get a look at the new yacht, and I couldn't think of anybody who wouldn't leave his or her grandmother's deathbed to take a ride on it, regardless of whether his or her lover or boyfriend or girlfriend or life partner could go along.

I'd been standing in the doorway, gaping, but now I realized that all the hairnet ladies who made our chocolates were also focused on the dramatic scene being played out in the break room. People were peeking around the doorway. They were craning their necks. Everyone wanted to see what was going on. I decided it was time for me to act like a boss.

"Brenda." I used my sternest voice. "Please go back to

work. Will, this is not a suitable time or place for this discussion. Please leave."

Apparently neither of them had been aware that I'd come in. They turned toward me in surprise. Will looked defiant, and I was afraid Brenda was going to cry.

But she didn't cry. She said, "I'll go as soon as I wash my face."

She held her chin high and walked out of the break room with more dignity than I had known she possessed. I heard the door to the restroom open and close.

Will hadn't moved. He was glaring after her. I spoke again, quietly this time. "I think you'd better go now, Will."

"I'm sorry I yelled, Lee."

"We'll survive. And, Will, if I were handing out invitations for the yacht outing, I'd give you one. But I didn't make up the guest list, and neither did Brenda."

"She got invited by that stupid little pipsqueak Byron Wendt!"

I realized that Brenda had been right. Will was jealous, but not of Marco Spear. He was jealous of Byron Wimp—I mean, Wendt. Which was completely ridiculous. I almost laughed.

"Will," I said, "goodness is sometimes rewarded."

"What do you mean?"

"Byron told Joe and me he gave Tracy and Brenda invitations because they were nice to him. I'm sure lots of girls aren't. He's not exactly anybody's dream man."

"Maybe not." Will gave a deep sigh. "Girls are sure funny."

"So are guys. Anyway, it's just an evening. Joe and I will keep an eye on Tracy and Brenda."

"Are you two going?"

"Oh, yes. Mr. Oxford sent us an invitation, and Joe wouldn't miss it."

"Well." Another deep sigh. "Please tell Brenda I apologize."

Will left by the back door.

Bless his heart. It is hard to be young. I had a miserable time being twenty.

I started for my office, but Aunt Nettie stopped me as I went through the workshop. "Lee, could you do an errand before you go back to work? We need Frangelico."

"Sure. I'll go right now."

I did a 180-degree turn and went back out the alley door. This wasn't a bad idea, I thought. If I was gone for a few minutes, Brenda could get her emotional act together without feeling that she had to answer to me in any way.

Frangelico is a hazelnut-flavored liqueur. Aunt Nettie uses it to make her fabulous Frangelico truffles ("a milk chocolate ball with hazelnut filling and sprinkled with tiny bits of nougat"). Those little round chocolates are among my favorites. They're right up there with Amaretto truffles ("a white chocolate ball filled with milk chocolate flavored with almond liqueur") or Jamaican rum truffles ("the ultimate dark chocolate truffle—dark rum–flavored filling coated with dark chocolate"). Hmm. Funny how my favorites are flavored with various alcoholic beverages. Drinking alcohol is okay, but it's more fun to eat it. Anyway, after the filling's been cooked, there's very little alcoholic content in Aunt Nettie's bonbons and truffles. They're not like the liqueur-filled chocolates some chocolatiers produce.

As I went out the door, I grabbed a chocolate from the discard bin—it looked like Dutch caramel, but I discovered the inside was raspberry cream, which explained why it was in the discard bin. I headed for the Superette, Warner Pier's one supermarket. It has a liquor department.

I rushed into the store, found my way to the liquor aisle, and plucked my bottle of Frangelico from the liqueur section. It was as I was leaving that I made a big step toward solving the mystery of the pirates of Warner Pier. Of course, I didn't realize it at the time.

To get from the liquor section to the checkout, I had to go past the books and magazines. And as I did, my eye fell on a copy of that biographical publication on Marco Spear, the one that my niece, Marcia Herrera, had shown me. I smiled, because Marcia is a delightful young lady, and her devotion to a movie star was so typical of being thirteen.

Then I wondered whether it was the same magazine. If it was a different one, Marcia might like a copy. I put my bottle of Frangelico down on top of a stack of *Martha Stewart Living* magazines and picked up the Marco mag. It was called, of course, *Marco!*

I leafed through it. There was a layout of photos on Marco at a series of movie premieres. Next came Marco at a rehearsal session, learning new sword-fighting routines, followed by a series of pictures of Marco with various minor actresses. Huh. I couldn't remember whether these were the same pictures Marcia had shown me. I headed for the back of the magazine. I remembered that Marcia's magazine had finished up with a layout of childhood pictures of Marco.

This one did, too, but some of the pictures weren't familiar. The magazine had school pictures of the athletic young actor—those awful mug shots that tortured us all in our grade school, middle school, and high school days. I was sure those weren't in Marcia's magazine.

And among them I found a picture of Marco at seventeen—just as plain as the rest of us, with squinty eyes and braces on his teeth.

I caught on. And I began to laugh. And I knew I couldn't tell a soul.

Except maybe Hogan. But I thought about it and decided he already knew.

I bought the magazine. If Marcia didn't want it, I did.

I headed back to the office, still chuckling. I wanted to get at least a little work done and still leave early. I didn't want to be late for my yacht trip.

When I went in the back door, I again heard Brenda. But this time she wasn't in the break room, and she wasn't yelling angrily. She was in the retail shop, and both she and Tracy were squealing.

They weren't acting like professional salespeople. I sped to the front.

"Tracy! Brenda! Settle down! You sound like a couple of piglets!"

"Lee! Lee! Look! Look!"

They were literally jumping up and down. They pulled me to the front window and pointed.

Traffic in front of the shop was busy, so busy that it had completely stopped. And there, right in front of TenHuis Chocolade, was an enormous limousine.

Tracy quit yelling. In fact, she almost whispered.

"He's really here," she said. "It's got to be Marco."

Chapter 18

"Back to work!"

I yelled the command.

I'd reached my limit on Marco Spear. I glared at Brenda and Tracy until they slunk back behind the counter.

"I'm only glad there were no customers present to see that little display," I said. "We do not know that Marco Spear is here or that he's even coming to Warner Pier. But whatever happens, I don't want any more screaming about it, even if he walks in the door and does a handspring."

Brenda and Tracy looked properly contrite and muttered apologies.

"If we don't have any customers," I said, "you two can start cleaning the shop."

I went into my office, then realized I still had the bottle of Frangelico in my hand, so I had to turn around and take it to Aunt Nettie before I settled down to work myself. I'd left the magazine in the van, thank goodness. I certainly wouldn't have liked for Tracy and Brenda to catch me with that.

But after I got to my desk, I found it hard to do anything.

The limousine had unsettled me as much as it had Tracy and Brenda, although not for the same reasons.

Was it there for Marco Spear?

A limo didn't necessarily mean a lot in Warner Pier. We have lots of wealthy summer residents who might make use of a limousine. True, they usually brought their more casual vehicles—the vintage Alfa Romeo or the Hummer—to Warner Pier. But I could think of several families who might have summoned a limousine to take them to meet the company jet in case they needed to fly someplace unexpectedly. Or maybe one of them had to attend a funeral, or a wedding, or do one of the dozens of other things that people who have all the money in the world use a limo for.

But, still . . . Was Marco making an official visit to Warner Pier? If he was, was Hogan aware of the situation? Did Hogan take seriously the notice that there was danger for Marco Spear in Warner Pier? Was he paying attention to that strange warning note someone had stuck in the TenHuis Chocolade door?

After all, some really odd things had happened. We had pirates, a man who had been shot to death and thrown in the lake, and another man who had disappeared. Plus, someone had tried to waylay Joe and me at the dock the night before. I couldn't ignore that, though I'd tried. If insignificant people like us were in danger, Marco Spear might be, too. After all, he was a valuable commodity. Photographers, publicity people, actors, makeup artists, whole movie studios and advertising agencies—thousands of people depended on him.

I could only guess why any of this was related to Marco Spear, but I was beginning to believe that it was.

I picked up the phone to call Hogan, then laid it down again. I'd discuss the situation with Joe before I did anything.

Joe was deeper in Hogan's confidence than I was. He and I could hash it out before the yacht trip, then contact Hogan if we needed to.

As soon as Brenda and Tracy were speaking to me again, I offered them a ride to Oxford Boats that evening. I was surprised at how readily they accepted. Then they asked what I was going to wear.

"I haven't quite decided," I said. "Casual, of course."

They nodded eagerly.

"But not jeans."

They frowned.

"At least not for me. I'm too old to wear jeans to a party."

"Oh, no, you're not, Lee," they lied.

I ignored that reply. "Rubber-soled shoes. Deck shoes or Top-Sider sandals, if you've got them. Or tennis shoes. We wouldn't want to mar the deck of that beautiful new yacht."

Nods.

"Jackets, because it might be cold out on the lake."

That drew nods, but accompanied by frowns. Jackets didn't sound glamorous to the college crowd.

I went on. "I guess I'll wear my good khaki slacks, my deck shoes, and a navy sweater. I'll carry my khaki canvas jacket over my arm. I think you girls will be fine in jeans or khakis, with sweaters or neat-looking sweatshirts. No messages across the bosoms. And bring jackets."

Tracy frowned. "It's just that we don't have time to buy anything."

"I really don't think this is a new-outfit occasion," I said. "The main thing to remember about any occasion is that you want to be comfortable, not concerned because your feet hurt or because you have to remember to hold your stomach in.

You want to be thinking about being interested in the yacht and talking to the other people on the trip, not worrying about how you look.

"And with that bit of philosophy from old Aunt Susanna Lee—I'll bet y'all didn't know Susanna is my first name—you two can go home. I'll watch the counter until Claire and Terri get here."

I didn't have to argue with them. They were out the door before I finished my sentence.

As soon as the two evening-shift girls arrived, I left, too. This might not be a new-outfit occasion, but I'd sure feel more festive if I had a shower before I went.

The shower was the reason I missed Joe. He came and went while I was underwater. So we didn't get a chance to discuss the threat to Marco Spear and how seriously Hogan was taking it. He just left a note, saying, "I've got to do a couple of things. Meet you at Oxford boatyard."

I picked up Tracy and Brenda, who seemed subdued but excited, and headed for the boatyard.

Brenda did say Will had left a message apologizing. "Oh," I said. I was staying out of that situation.

So it was a little bit surprising when the person who let us in the gate at Oxford Boats was Will.

We all squawked his name. "Will!"

He grinned. The guy did have a winning grin. "Hi, ladies," he said. "Guess what? I snagged an invitation, too."

"How?" Brenda sounded excited.

"I'm just a worker bee. My boss talked to the Oxford foreman and found out they could use another crewman tonight. He gave them a vastly overrated account of my skills as a sailor, and I'm on as a deckhand and car parker."

We parked where Will directed, gathered up our jackets, and went to meet Joe, who introduced us to Charles Oxford, owner of Oxford Boats. Mr. Oxford—nobody called him Charles that night—has a home in Warner Pier but mainly lives in Chicago. He was a distinguished-looking older guy with the dignified presence he would need to deal with celebrity and wealthy clients. He seemed to awe Brenda and Tracy, and maybe he awed me, too.

Then we stepped on board the yacht. And who was already on board but Aunt Nettie and Hogan? We greeted them. Then Byron appeared, looking unusually wimpy. It seemed that his teeth were more bucked than ever, that his glasses were thicker, and that his accent sounded dumber. I was proud of Tracy and Brenda. When he offered to give us a tour, neither of them looked around for a better-looking guide.

The tour was fabulous because the yacht was fabulous. It had an aft deck that was larger than my living room. It featured a long built-in couch—it would seat at least seven—plus several other chairs and tables, all covered with all-weather fabric.

Then Byron led us up a flight of cantilevered stairs—sorry, I have trouble calling something so sleekly designed a "companionway"—to the fly deck, the deck way up on top. That was twice the size of the aft deck and so high that it felt as if it should give the passengers a view of Wisconsin. Actually, even that tall a deck wouldn't let us see more than eight miles, so Wisconsin was still a hundred miles out of range. But we felt—well, way up high.

For more intimate chitchat, there was a forward deck out on the bow with seating for, say, half a dozen.

Then we followed Byron inside. We saw the lower-deck

salon, the galley, and the gym. We saw the five guest cabins, each with private bath, and the master suite, which stretched the full twenty-five-foot width of the yacht and included a sitting room. We skipped lightly over the engine room, the bridge, the radar and sonar, the "garage" where Jet Skis or a dinghy could be stored, the water makers—to convert seawater to fresh when the yacht was in an ocean—the air-conditioning and heating, and the water wings. Or I guess it had water wings. It had everything else.

By the time Byron escorted us to the main salon—another twenty-five-foot-wide, ultradecorated room—I was beyond amazement. The bar and buffet table were set up in the main salon, and I headed for them. I shouldered my way through a half dozen people who were already standing around the bar without looking at the other guests.

The bartender—I recognized him as a Herrera Catering employee—held up a pitcher of red liquid. "Sangria?"

"Sounds good," I said. "I don't think I've seen sangria since I left Texas."

"It hasn't been 'in' around here," the bartender said. "Maybe this will inspire a revival."

The person next to me tapped me on the shoulder. "Hi, Lee," he said. "I'd ask you what you're doing here, but I don't even know what I'm doing here."

It was Chuck O'Riley, editor of the *Warner Pier Gazette*.

I smiled. "Why shouldn't you be here, Chuck? You certainly have as much right as I do."

"I'm in pretty impressive company," Chuck said. "Way out of my depth."

He gestured, and at the same time another person spoke. "Well, if it isn't Mrs. Woodyard."

It was Gordon Hitchcock, with LMTV News. The television reporter I love to hate.

Gordon and I have bumped heads on several occasions. I nodded and started to move away from him. Then I saw the man behind him, and I recognized him, too. I don't know his name, but three years earlier—when Joe was having a lot of trouble with the sensational press after his first wife was murdered—that guy had been a correspondent for one of the racier tabloids, and he'd nearly driven Joe insane. I didn't know the fourth man, but somehow I wasn't surprised when Chuck told me he was from the Associated Press.

But it was the fifth man, the one who was urging all the reporters to dig into the buffet, who was dominating the crowd at the bar. He was dressed flashy, and he acted flashy. His hair was an unnatural blond, and his eyes were an unnatural blue. He talked a lot and smiled even more. He was, Chuck said, a representative of Marco Spear. A press agent.

Joe and I had been invited to the press peek.

Oh, ye gods! I wondered whether Joe knew. He had made his way to the bridge, since he was more interested in the mechanical aspects of the yacht than in the gym, the galley, and the guest cabins.

I hoped he stayed there.

I clutched my sangria and headed for the upper deck at top speed.

As I went by Brenda and Tracy, I grabbed them and pulled them aside. I warned both of them not to speak to anyone in the group at the bar and buffet.

"They're press," I said. "I don't think they're interested in Joe or me. I'm sure they're here to check out Marco Spear's yacht. But you both know the problems we've had with reporters in the past, so please, please—don't talk to them at all. Don't answer the most innocent question."

About that time, the captain came over the intercom system and told us where to find life jackets. The yacht gave a honk, and it left its berth. We were off.

We moved slowly out into the river and toward the lake. There were even more boats out to gawk that evening than there had been the evening before. Joe continued to be among the missing, and I was sure he was looking over the mechanical parts of the yacht.

I was still nervous about the reporters, so I grabbed Aunt Nettie, who can turn a reporter into an ally with her smile, and the two of us sat down on the aft deck.

The yacht moved down the river. Byron had become a waiter, and he brought us each a plate of goodies. We jokingly did the Queen Elizabeth II wave at the boats following the yacht, especially if we saw someone we knew. We moved around the deck, looking the vessel over. I also counted heads and realized that there were only about a dozen people on board, plus four or five crew members.

There were the four reporters and the press agent. Gordon Hitchcock hadn't even been allowed to bring a photographer. Then there were Aunt Nettie, Hogan, Brenda, Tracy, Joe, me, and some guy who looked familiar but whom I couldn't identify. He and Hogan were hanging out.

After my initial upset over the reporters being on the excursion, I was again looking forward to the trip.

Then we went through the channel and out into Lake Michigan. Our flotilla of small boats—actually some of them were thirty- or fifty-footers—came with us. As it had the night before, the big yacht seemed to preen, posing for her admirers for five or ten minutes. Then she put on the speed and left them all bouncing in her wake. Most fell behind and went back into Warner Pier, though I could still see the running lights of a few. By then the sun was down, and it was getting dark.

The lake wasn't rough, and I was enjoying myself thoroughly. The yacht turned north, toward Holland, and traveled along parallel to the shore. After about five miles, it slowed and almost came to a halt.

Joe and Hogan came down from the bridge and joined Aunt Nettie and me.

I smiled at Joe. "What do you think of her?"

"A very neat craft," he said.

The words had just left his mouth when the pirates came up the aft gangway.

Chapter 19

The first pirate was dressed like the one who had boarded Joe's boat back in June, but it wasn't the same man. Not unless he'd put on several pounds over the summer. This one had quite a paunch.

No, he might have the black beard, the bandana, and the golden earring, but he wasn't nearly as sexy as the other pirate had been. Definitely not the same guy.

Of course, I might have thought that because I was convinced the first pirate had been Hal Weldon, and Hal was dead.

The pirate spun around on one leg in a dance move. Then he cried out, "Aha, me hearties! Shiver me timbers!" He began to prance around, but he didn't do any handstands or make any other athletic moves. He did have a certain pizzazz, but he definitely wasn't athletic enough to walk on his hands on the gunwale of Joe's boat.

People were applauding him, and the applause grew as two more pirates came over the stern. Again there was a sexy pirate queen, accompanied by a smaller pirate who carried a pipe. The piper began to pipe, and the costumed girl began to dance. I thought she was the same pirate queen who had boarded us on Midsummer's Eve. I concentrated on watching their performance.

The yacht had quite an advantage over Joe's boat. The entertainers had room to move around vigorously, and they did. The girl not only danced; she did roundoffs and aerial cartwheels. The piper lost the tune a couple of times, but he kicked up his heels enthusiastically.

I looked at him critically. Was this the same guy who had played the pennywhistle aboard Joe's boat?

But it didn't matter. The first pirate had disappeared back down the companionway that led to the swim platform, so the pirate queen and the piper had the aft deck all to themselves. They were having fun. All the passengers and crew were having fun. Or so I thought. I looked around for crew members. I could see the captain and another crew member up on the top deck—they were leaning over the railing to see the show. The reporters who had been in the main salon were up there, too. Will was standing at the back of the aft deck, near Brenda and Tracy. They were clapping in time to the music. Aunt Nettie, Joe—they were laughing together. Hogan and the stranger were near each other. I saw them exchanging a look, but they were both grinning.

Who wasn't there?

It was Byron, I realized. There was no sign of him. But that was just from my point of view. The yacht was so large that Byron might have had a wonderful spot for watching the performance.

The antics went on for around five minutes before the lead pirate, the first one over the railing, reappeared. He waved his arms and called for silence.

Then he spoke in a raspy pirate-type voice. "Bring out the treasure!"

The queen and the piper ran back down the companion-way to the swim platform. Standing up so that I could get a view of what was going on, I could see that their inflatable boat was tied up there. The two lifted out a large box decorated to look like a pirate chest. A fourth pirate had stayed in the inflatable, and he helped them lift it; it seemed to be quite heavy.

The three of them carried the chest up to the aft deck, seeming to stagger under its weight. Then, with flourishes from all four pirates, they opened the lid.

A dozen helium balloons floated out.

Yes, it got a big laugh from all of us.

They proceeded to do several more stunts with the box. A half dozen pigeons flew out, and the pirates all jumped back and two of them did pratfalls. They put the girl in it, waved a colorful cloth around, and tried to get her to disappear. Except that she didn't. We all laughed hard at that. They produced necklaces and other jewelry from the chest—the type that people bring home from Mardi Gras—and they threw them to all of us. I caught a purple one, then a gold, and draped them around my neck. Aunt Nettie caught red and blue beads.

It was by far the most elaborate pirate show that I'd heard of all summer. It went on longer and had more parts and in-volved props—the chest, the birds, the balloons, the beads—that the other boardings hadn't used. It also had more people performing. But after all, the large yacht gave them more room. It was logical that they were using it.

It was probably ten minutes before the pirate queen cer-emoniously closed the lid to the chest, did another cartwheel, and skipped lightly down the aft companionway. She got into the inflatable and held it steady. The two men carried the chest down to the dinghy and loaded it aboard. While they were doing this, the pirate king did a few more dance moves and yelled, "Yo-ho-ho!" He didn't board the inflatable until its outboard motor roared.

We were all cheering as the boat sped off. The only odd thing was that after about a quarter mile, the pirates cut their running lights. Basically, they disappeared into the dark. This is not legal, but none of us called the Coast Guard.

Hogan was standing near Aunt Nettie and me. "Hey," I said, "if there's any reason you want to know where those guys go, the captain of this thing could watch them on radar."

Hogan smiled smugly. "We've thought of that."

"I guess it doesn't matter," I said, "since they don't seem to commit any crimes during their escapades."

"Yes, but when people are running around my town in disguise, I always like to know who they are."

It was at precisely that moment when the man I didn't know, the one who had been muttering with Hogan off and on for the whole cruise, leaned over the fly-deck railing and called out.

"Hogan! We need you up here."

Hogan took off up the companionway at top speed. I craned my neck, trying to see what was going on up there, and Joe did, too.

By that time it was pretty dark. Only a narrow band of orange remained in the western sky.

There were lights all over the yacht, of course, but we were out on Lake Michigan. Outdoors, that is. Even good lighting doesn't seem to illuminate things outdoors. There are no walls for it to bounce off to enclose it. Even bright lighting seems to be soaked up by the darkness that surrounds it outdoors.

I looked up at the fly deck, and I couldn't see a thing. And suddenly I was frightened. I grabbed Joe's arm. "Where's Byron?"

"Byron?" He sounded surprised. "Why do you want Byron?"

"I just want to be sure he's all right."

"All right? Why shouldn't he be all right?"

I shook my head. "Maybe he's still at the bar."

I went into the lower salon and took the companionway up to the main salon. The reporters were gathered around the bar, and for a moment I felt reassured. Byron must be handing out drinks. Then heads parted, and I saw that Will was acting as bartender.

I went over to the bar. "Will! Where's Byron?"

"I don't know. He disappeared, the jerk. The steward told me to take over. I don't know what I'm doing."

I briefly felt sorry for him. Will had always done mechanical jobs. He'd worked with cars, and now with boats. He definitely wasn't the waiter-bartender type.

"Let me look for Byron for a moment," I said. "Then I'll come and help you."

Will's glance was grateful.

I turned around to see Hogan come partway down the interior companionway from the fly deck and gesture to Joe. When Joe approached him, they conferred. Joe shook his head. I couldn't hear what Joe said, but I could hear an angry voice from up above. It sounded like Charles Oxford.

We must have some mechanical problem. That would infuriate any yacht builder. Here he takes the press out on the snazzy new yacht, and it develops a glitch. I might have laughed if it hadn't been for the scared feeling in the pit of my stomach.

But why should I be scared? Even if we had a mechanical problem, the yacht was perfectly safe. This was no sleazy tramp steamer registered in some Podunk country. This was one of the most technically advanced boats in the world, loaded with safety features.

I kept looking for Byron. I checked the gym, the staterooms, the galley. I ran up and down companionways and back and forth on decks. I looked behind furniture—feeling stupid—and under plants. I walked up the companionway leading to the fly deck. I didn't quite have the nerve to go up there and join the mechanical crew. I stopped with my head just above the level of the floor and counted heads. I saw no one but crew members, Hogan, Joe, and Hogan's pal. They all looked concerned. I came down and looked some more.

It crossed my mind that I might find Byron in an embarrassing position, and he wouldn't appreciate my search. But I kept searching anyway.

But I didn't find our wimpy pal anywhere.

I finally decided I was going to have to ask someone about him.

Who? Charles Oxford was in charge, of course, but I could still hear his voice rumbling unhappily up on the fly deck. In fact, the whole crew seemed to be up there—plus Hogan, Joe, and Hogan's friend.

Then I saw the blond public relations guy. He was still shepherding press around. I boldly walked into the group and touched his arm. He whipped his head around, surprised.

"Sorry to bother you," I said. "I have a rather important question."

That's one of the advantages of being tall. When you act firm, people tend to obey. I led him away from the press corps and introduced myself.

He grinned. "I'm Daren Roberts," he said. "I'm with Majestic Studios."

I nodded. "I wondered if you know where Byron is."

"Byron?" His voice was wary.

I tried to make my voice firm. "Byron."

"Oh, I'm sure he's around somewhere."

"Yes, I'm sure he is. But where is that somewhere? Frankly, I've looked all over the craft."

"Why do you need to know?"

"I'm uneasy about his safety."

Daren Roberts and I looked into each other's eyes for a long moment. Then he spoke. "What did he tell you?"

"He didn't tell me anything, but I'm a good guesser."

He laughed derisively.

"And," I said, "my thirteen-year-old niece insisted that I read a magazine with lots of old pictures in it."

The derisive laugh turned to a cough.

"So where is he?"

He whispered. "He could be locked in the main cabin with a nubile young woman."

"I looked there. Plus, the only nubile young women on board are my stepsister and her friend, and they're both standing right over there with my aunt."

"Oh." Daren looked around the salon. "Well, I'm sure everything is all right. But I'll look for him."

I had to be content with that for the moment. Daren walked off, looking worried, and I joined Brenda and Tracy.

Tracy leaned close to me. "Is there some problem with the boat?"

"Maybe, but I'm sure it's not serious."

"Will says it's something with the radar."

"Could be."

Brenda's eyes were big. "It's not . . . not dangerous, is it?"

I smiled at her. "Well, they haven't broken out the lifeboats."

That didn't seem to reassure her, so I patted her arm. "Brenda, people sailed all over the oceans for thousands of years without radar. As long as we have a compass, we can find the shore. We're only a few miles out."

"Miles?"

"Maybe two or three. To get home we go straight east until we see a light, okay? Then the captain knows where he is, and we head north or south until he sees the lighthouse at the entrance to the Warner River. We still have lights. Nothing's been said about the radio being out. We're fine."

She nodded. "I knew everything was all right."

"After all, this is a test cruise. The equipment is still being broken in."

But that radar ought to be working, I knew. I didn't say anything more.

Joe came down from the fly deck then. He was frowning. I grabbed him as he went by.

"What's the problem?" I said.

Joe lowered his voice. "The radar's gone out."

"So they weren't able to figure out where the pirates went."

"Among other things."

He moved, but I kept hold of his arm.

"Have they found Byron?"

"I didn't know anyone was looking for him."

"I have been. He hasn't been around since the pirates left."

"So?"

"Oh, come on, Joe! Surely Hogan told you."

"Told me what?"

"Byron!"

"What about him?"

"Joe! Byron is Marco Spear!"

Chapter 20

Joe laughed. "Okay, Lee! You got it. But don't get too excited."

"Why not?"

"He hasn't fallen overboard."

"Then where is he?"

Joe moved his lips close to my ear. "It's a publicity stunt."

I stood still, without moving. I didn't know if I should be happy or sad. I was relieved, but I felt like a complete fool.

Of course! We were talking about a movie star! What was more logical than a publicity stunt? It made perfect sense.

For a moment.

Then I didn't quite believe it. I kept my hold on Joe's arm. "The warnings? The publicity people sent those? They called Byron's mom? They stuck a strange note in the shop's door?"

"I suppose so. Or maybe Byron's mom is part of the plan."

"What about the dead man? Hal Weldon?"

"He didn't have anything to do with Byron."

"Yes, he did. Through Jeremy."

"Jeremy?"

"Yes. Jeremy called Byron's mom, and Byron told us he'd

known Jeremy in high school. So there's a connection between Jeremy and Marco. And that means there's a connection between Marco and Hal."

"What connection?"

"Jeremy!"

"Pretty far-fetched, Lee."

"Jeremy and Hal knew each other. And you'll never get me to believe that Jeremy disappeared off the same beach where Hal's body was found"—I emphasized the next words—"by coincidence. Jeremy pulled that drowning stunt to force a search of the area so Hal's body would be found."

Joe sighed. "You'll have to talk to Hogan." He led me toward the companionway going up to the fly deck.

I'd already looked at the scene up there, of course, and things hadn't changed since I'd peeked earlier. The fly deck—the top of the yacht—was brightly lit. Charles Oxford, the captain, and another crewman were huddled over the controls at the bridge. The yacht was moving gently through the water—not very fast—and I could see lights on the horizon straight ahead. Apparently we were headed back toward shore, whether the radar was working or not.

Hogan was standing against the rear railing, and Joe led me to him.

"Hogan, Lee's got some questions," he said. He lowered his voice. "She's figured out who Byron is, for one thing."

Hogan grinned, and when he spoke he also kept his voice low. "Then you know he's the owner of this boat."

"Who he is isn't the question, Hogan," I said. "It's where he is. I don't believe he's on the yacht."

"Then it seems as if things are going according to plan."

"Whose plan?"

"Some Hollywood publicity type. When I went out to talk to the people at Oxford Boats, they pulled the so-called Byron in, and he explained the whole deal. And it's a publicity stunt."

"What's he getting publicity for?"

"His next movie. It seems the critics didn't like his performance in *Young Blackbeard*."

"I read a few of the reviews. They liked the leaping around and the sword fighting, but they didn't think much of his acting."

"Right. So Marco—his dad's name was Byron and his mother's maiden name was Wendt—got mad. His role in this next movie is going to require real acting."

"I read about that, too. He's going to play a sickly guy who's not too bright."

"Yep. So he decided to try the role out in real life."

"You're kidding!"

Hogan held up a finger in shushing position. "It's true. He came to Warner Pier—well, because he wanted to see the yacht he'd ordered—but also because he wanted to 'immerse himself' in the new role. Or that's what he told me."

"So he assumed the role of Byron Wimp. I mean, Wendt."

Hogan nodded.

"I will say he did a good job," I said. "I thought Byron was the squirrelliest character I'd run into in a long time."

"But Joe says you figured out who he really was. How'd you do it?"

"I picked up one of the biographical magazines on Marco Spear, just wondering if Marcia would like a copy. It has a high school picture of him in it, and the picture was a dead ringer for Byron Wendt. Glasses. Terrible haircut. Except for the buckteeth. He had braces in those days. The teeth must be an appliance he got from the makeup department."

Joe and Hogan laughed.

"Then I began to remember some things," I said. "Such as when Byron fell off his bicycle in Joe's lane, he curled into a ball and rolled."

"The way a gymnast would?"

"Yes. And when Aunt Nettie's fancy pirate ship nearly fell over, he slipped around like a snake and grabbed it. He has superb coordination. Plus, he told us he was low man on the totem pole at Oxford Boats, but he managed to leave whenever he wanted to, and he was supposedly given permission to invite guests for tonight's cruise. Things like that."

"You didn't tell anybody?"

"No. I figured he wanted it to be a surprise, and I didn't want to ruin his plan. But after the pirates came on board I couldn't find him. So I did ask that Hollywood guy, Daren Roberts, to look for him."

Hogan nodded. "Roberts has been hanging around the yacht a lot. He should know the layout, so surely he can find him. I'm sure Byron is somewhere on board. He was going to announce who he was after we got back to the boatyard, then take off for Hollywood in the limo that drove down Peach Street this afternoon. He's probably changing back to his real identity. Getting rid of the teeth and so on."

"I hope you're right."

I leaned back against the railing and watched the activity on the bridge. The yacht had two control stations—this one on the fly deck and an identical one down in the main salon. The two were linked, and whatever commands were given at one were copied at the other. Of course, only one of them functioned at a time. The captain and another crewman were watching the sophisticated gauges and equipment that ran this luxury yacht.

It was cool up there, and I'd left my jacket two levels down, on the aft deck. I thought of going to get it, but I didn't want to miss anything. There was definitely a lot happening on the fly deck.

Charles Oxford was as mad as hops, as I'd deduced from the loud talk I'd heard earlier, but he'd stopped yelling. He walked over to Hogan and spoke.

"Some jerk cut the power to the radar controls. I'll never allow another reporter on one of my crafts."

Hogan looked quizzical. "Why would one of the reporters damage the yacht?"

"Just to be obnoxious." I expected him to declare the reporters a "scurvy lot," or use some other sea-dog expression to describe them. And maybe he would have, except that Daren Roberts came running up the companionway.

As soon as he got to the top, he came to an abrupt halt and looked carefully all around the fly deck. When he saw our little group, he walked toward us, pulling out a handkerchief and wiping his forehead as he came.

"You're right, Mrs. Woodyard," he said. "I can't find Byron anyplace."

Oxford erupted. "What! He's hiding someplace. Being funny."

Roberts' face was a picture of misery. "I hope you're right. Apparently no one's seen him since the pirates came on board."

"We'll see about that." Oxford strode to the controls and picked up a microphone. "Byron Wendt," the loudspeakers roared. "Byron Wendt. Report to the fly bridge. On the double."

The voice on the sound system left no room for dillydallying. Byron was to report right that minute. We all looked at the companionway, waiting for Byron's head to appear, listening for his feet to pound as they ran up the cantilevered stairs.

But Byron didn't come. Nothing happened.

Oxford waited about three minutes, then gave his preemptory summons again. Again, nothing happened.

The mood changed subtly. While Oxford was still stamping around, obviously angry, there was now an element of unease in his actions.

I could understand why. If he'd taken a teen idol out on one of his yachts and failed to bring him back—well, the publicity was going to be worldwide, and it wasn't going to be good.

Especially when there were hundreds of square miles of Lake Michigan surrounding the yacht. Oxford and his captain had to face the possibility that the owner of this multimillion-dollar yacht had fallen overboard.

But I didn't think Byron had gone into the drink. I thought he'd gone off with the pirates. The last time I saw him—and I admit I was keeping an eye on our famous host—was just before the pirates came on board. I thought he'd left with them.

The question was, had he gone willingly?

Had Marco Spear left with the pirates as part of a publicity stunt? Or were the warnings true? Had there been danger to him? Had he been taken against his will?

On that one I wasn't willing to guess. The whole thing could be another hoax like the one I felt sure Jeremy had pulled. Or the pirates might have actually kidnapped Byron—Marco—somehow.

But how? The four pirates had had the continuous attention of a dozen people during the whole time they were on board the yacht.

I went over the whole thing in my mind. Where had I last seen Byron?

He'd brought around some cheese and crackers when Aunt Nettie and I were on the aft deck. He'd gone all around the deck like a good waiter, and he'd been lingering near the aft companionway just before the first pirate came up it.

At that point my attention had shifted to the pirate, and I had no further recollection of Byron. Had he moved back onto the deck, toward the salon? I didn't think so. As far as I was concerned, Byron had disappeared right at the top of the companionway—or the stairs, as we landlubbers would say—the stairs that led down to the swim platform.

That platform was itself a little deck, a deck very close to water level. It was where swimmers would climb off and on the yacht. If was where Jet Skis or a dinghy would be launched or hauled aboard. It was where the "garage," the compartment for storing those items, was accessed.

If—big if—Byron was planning to leave the yacht with the pirates, it would be the logical place for him to wait to get aboard their inflatable.

But when the pirates did leave, Byron hadn't been with them. We'd all rushed to look at them as they'd loaded their equipment into the raft, started their outboard motor, waved, and rode off into the dark.

Equipment. Hmm. I thought about that. Their equipment

had included the magic pirate chest. People could get in a chest like that one and disappear.

"Oh, rats!" I said it out loud. "Byron left in the pirate's treasure chest. The jerk! He had to get in willingly. He's scared us just as a stunt."

I whirled around, looking for Hogan, ready to share my deduction, a deduction that Hogan had probably already made.

Now Hogan—and Joe—had joined Charles Oxford and the yacht's captain at the helm. And the radio was making noise.

When I touched Hogan's arm and tried to talk to him, he shushed me firmly. He was listening to the radio, and he didn't want to talk to me.

I couldn't understand it at first. Then a word caught my ear.

"Kidnapped!"

I listened harder.

"We have your movie star," the voice on the radio said. "He's safe, and he'll stay safe as long as you do what we say. But we want twenty million dollars for him."

Chocolate Chat
Chocolate Might Become Fuel

British scientists are testing a plan that would see the waste from chocolate factories used as fuel—for a race car.

The car runs on a mixture of vegetable oils and chocolate waste.

Researchers at the University of Warwick claim their car is the fastest vehicle yet to run on biofuels. Many parts of the car are also made from plant fibers. The steering wheel, for example, is made from fibers that come from carrots, and the seat is made from flax.

The builders say it meets Formula 3 specifications for size, weight, and performance. They hope it will reach speeds as high as 145 miles per hour.

The scientists maintain that their project proves that an efficient and speedy car can also be environmentally friendly.

Chapter 21

I knew a little more by the time we got back up the Warner River and docked at Oxford Boats.

Someone had called the Oxford Boats phone with the message about Marco being kidnapped. The people on duty there had relayed the message to the yacht by radio, and, of course, our search had confirmed that Marco Spear was not on the yacht.

The Michigan State Police were already checking on the phone that had sent the original message, but it was a cell phone, and no one had any real hope that the number would lead to anything. It's too easy to buy a temporary phone anonymously.

So the yacht headed in with a glum group of passengers aboard. Even the reporters seemed to share the general mood of dismay; they were excited, but not in a happy way. I believe that if one of them had made a cynical comment, the rest of the passengers—those of us who knew Marco in his persona as Byron—would have thrown him overboard. Without a life jacket.

Some people, including me, considered the idea that this

was a publicity stunt, that Marco hadn't really been kidnapped. But the near hysteria of Daren Roberts convinced me that it was true.

Roberts kept yanking his cell phone out, looking at it, then jamming it back in his pocket. Fifteen seconds later he'd do the same thing over again. He was pacing back and forth, looking toward the shore, obviously desperate to get back to the boatyard.

"I can't believe I don't have service out here," he said. His voice was close to a wail.

We were at the dock before the reporters were able to get sense out of Roberts.

"Why should we believe that this isn't a publicity stunt?" Chuck O'Riley asked the question.

"It was to be a publicity stunt," Roberts said. "Not the kidnapping, of course. Marco planned the whole thing himself. He was to establish himself here in Warner Pier as this other person, Byron Wendt. Then, tonight he wanted to invite people he'd met here, plus some press reps. He'd give tours and serve drinks, still pretending to be Byron Wendt. And after he was sure that everybody thought he was really that guy, I was to announce that Marco was on board. And then he'd pop up. He planned to do a handstand on the top deck"—Daren motioned toward the fly deck—"then walk on his hands down those stairs." He pointed toward the companionway leading from the aft deck to the fly deck. "But I never got the signal to make the announcement."

"How did the pirates who boarded the ship fit in?"

"They didn't! We tried to get in touch with them. We thought they would be a neat addition to the whole plan. But none of us could find them."

"Will the studio pay the ransom?"

Daren waved questions aside. "That's not my decision! I've got to get to a real phone!" He ran down the aft companionway and jumped onto the dock.

Brenda and Tracy had eyes the size of tennis balls. I guess I did, too.

"Byron was Marco?" Tracy sounded almost stunned.

I nodded.

Brenda spoke in a faint voice. "But why did he invite us along on the yacht?"

I put an arm around each of them. "Because whenever Byron came in the shop, you two were nice to him, even though he was playing the part of a real nerd that no girl would be interested in."

"Oh." They sounded unbelieving.

"There's a moral in there someplace, I guess. I'm not sure what it is." I led them to seats in the salon. "Stick with me, kids. We'll probably have to answer a lot of questions before we can leave."

But we didn't. The state police met us at the dock, but there weren't enough cops available to quiz all the bystanders. They took everybody's phone number and told us to go home. Will had to stay and help tuck the yacht in for the night, but Aunt Nettie left along with me. Since Hogan was a law officer who had witnessed the kidnapping, he was staying at the boatyard. Joe would come in his truck.

Before we left, Hogan spoke to the group, asking the rest of us not to say anything about the kidnapping.

"It probably won't be kept secret," he said. "But for the moment, let's keep it quiet. It won't be easy, I know, but think how you'd feel if you were the one who leaked the news and Marco Spear was killed by the kidnappers."

That did make Brenda and Tracy look awed. A big tear oozed out of Tracy's left eye.

As we stepped onto the dock, I could hear the reporters haranguing Hogan. Keeping the kidnapping quiet wasn't going to be easy. Maybe not even possible.

When Aunt Nettie, Brenda, Tracy, and I were in the van, I looked at my watch. To my astonishment, it was only nine o'clock. So much had happened since we went on board that I felt like it ought to be midnight.

But one thing that hadn't happened was dinner.

"I know I should be home wringing my hands," I said. "And I am upset. But I'm also hungry. How about a pizza?"

Everybody fell in with that idea. We called various boyfriends and husbands—it was good to be on shore and have decent cell phone service. Will and Carl, Tracy's boyfriend, promised to join us when they could, and Joe said he'd meet us, too. We drove to the Dock Street Pizza Place, Warner Pier's contribution to that all-American, Italian-inspired fun food, and we were able to shove two tables together to seat a party of seven. We ordered, and Joe, Will, and Carl had all arrived by the time the pizza was on the table.

We were all chewing when the theater crowd walked in.

In this case, the "theater crowd" was the cast and crew members from the Showboat Theater, rather than people who had attended a play. There were no performances that week. Rehearsals were going on for *The Pirates of Penzance*.

There were eight in their group, and I was surprised at how many I knew. Maggie and Ken McNutt were there, and Max Morgan and Mikki White. There were another four people I didn't know but had seen on stage. The waitress moved two tables together to accommodate them, so between the two groups—them and us—we'd taken over the center of the small restaurant.

Maggie and Ken stopped to speak to us on the way in, and after their group had given its order, Max got up and walked around the tables to speak to Joe and me.

"Did I hear that you two went out on the new yacht?"

"Yes, we were lucky enough to get an invitation," Joe said.

"Pretty impressive, I imagine."

"I'd call it spectacular."

Max leaned closer and lowered his voice. "That weird guy was back tonight. The one I think is from Chicago. He was looking for Jeremy again."

"The man you thought might be a loan shark?"

"Right." Max frowned. "He's a real strange one."

"Did you call the cops?"

"What can I tell them? We have a patron who creeps me out? That's not a crime. Besides, I already told the local gendarmes about him."

"What did he do this time?"

"We were rehearsing the first-act finale. I looked up, and there he was, sitting in the back row, just watching. I felt, you know, as if I had to assert myself, so at the end of the scene I walked back there and told him to leave."

"Did he?"

"First he quizzed me about Jeremy again. Had we heard from him? Was the search continuing?"

"But he did leave?"

"Yes. But he did it . . . insolently."

"Did you get his license number?"

"No. I followed him to the door, but I couldn't read it. He'd covered it up some way."

"I think you should talk to Hogan about the episode. The search for Jeremy is still going on."

"Surely the guy will quit coming around when he figures out that Jeremy is gone for good."

"You think Jeremy is dead?"

"Oh, no! I'm convinced Jeremy knew the Chicago guy was after him and took off for parts unknown." Max knelt beside Joe. "Meanwhile, I'm glad you two had a nice evening. Did the Oxford people confirm that the new yacht belongs to Marco Spear?"

"Not in so many words."

Max shrugged. "Still, a few hors d'oeuvres, a pitcher of something cold and exotic, and a cruise are worth something."

He rejoined his own group.

I muttered to Joe, "Are you still skeptical about this so-called loan shark?"

"Yep."

We ate pizza and talked with our group for the next twenty minutes. Everyone kept their voices low, of course. Carl had to be told about the kidnapping, but Tracy swore him to secrecy. I didn't have much hope that the news wouldn't get out. When more than a dozen people knew—and five of them were newsmen—there simply wasn't a hope. But I didn't want to be the one who blew it.

So when I saw Mikki coming around the table, apparently planning to speak to me, I hurriedly poked Brenda as a hint that she should change the subject.

I was still angry with Mikki for giving me the runaround

when I went to the theater trying to pick Jill up. I spoke to her, but I didn't exactly gush out a welcome.

"Hi, Mikki. Has Jill turned up?"

"No, but she's supposed to be back tomorrow." She knelt beside my chair. "I'm sorry, Ms. Woodyard. I apologize for all that. Jill asked me to do it."

"Why?"

"She said she needed to meet someone. She didn't want to give the police chief a big explanation. She went out the front while I kept you in the back."

"She could have told me. Hogan was just trying to save her embarrassment by sending me to pick her up, instead of a patrol car."

"Well, I wanted to apologize to you."

"Apology accepted," I said. I kept the word "maybe" to myself. It was time to change the subject.

"You're working on *The Pirates of Penzance* now, aren't you? How are your rehearsals going?"

"Tonight was underwear. I mean, understudies."

I managed not to laugh. Again I realized that Mikki had the same affliction I do.

"I'm understudying Jill as Mabel," she said. "Mostly I'm one of the cousins. Tonight was kind of different, since Maggie was in charge."

"Oh? I didn't know she was taking that important a part."

"She doesn't usually. But she's really good. Of course, the play's a lot of fun. But Max wants us to play it straight."

"Straight?"

"Yes, he says it's funnier that way."

I racked my brain for something to say about Gilbert and

Sullivan. "I guess it's hard not to make a play that old seem dated."

"The lines are very clever. Max says it's important for it not to be campy . . ." To my surprise, Mikki's face grew red. Was she blushing? But she went on talking. "I mean, well, Max wants it straight."

She blinked rapidly. "Hal's folks came today. You know, to get him. Take him home. I felt really sorry for them."

I nodded. I felt sorry for them, too. Sorry enough that I tried to change the subject again.

"Has anybody figured out where Hal was working after he left the theater in June?"

"Not that I know of. Our food's here. Guess I'd better go." She stood up.

I spoke. "Thanks for the piecemeal—I mean, peacemaking!" Now I'd done it. Tangled my tongue. Mikki and I might be twins. "Thanks for the peacemaking gesture."

Mikki looked pained. "I shouldn't have let Jill talk me into it. I don't mean to be campy . . ." Mikki's face flamed. It was more than a blush; it was a conflagration. She turned a brilliant scarlet. "I mean, catty! I didn't mean to be catty."

She muttered a few more words and went back to her own table, where pizzas were being served.

Her remarks had left me with a sense that I'd missed something. Something she'd said had tickled some memory deep in my brain, but I couldn't get the memory to surface. I went into a fog, trying to figure it out.

We worked on our own pizzas for a while, and Brenda and Will had another of their arguments about Marco Spear's acting ability. I was so deep in my own thoughts that I ignored them until Brenda said, "I would think, Will, that tonight of all nights—"

"Brenda!" I hissed the word, afraid she was going to blurt out something about the kidnapping within earshot of the theater crowd at the next table. After that narrow escape, we all fell so silent that when my cell phone rang the sound made me jump.

I nearly threw the phone to the floor trying to dig it out of my purse and look at it. Hogan was calling. "Lee? Is Nettie with you?"

"Yes. We all went out to get something to eat."

"Where the hell are you?"

I looked at the phone with raised eyebrows. Hogan never swore. He must be really upset.

"We're at the Dock Street, Hogan. Do you want us to meet you somewhere?"

"No. I'll come there."

He hung up.

I told Aunt Nettie he was on the way; then I quietly described the call to Joe. "I've never heard him so mad, Joe. Annoyed, yes. But this time he was really angry."

"Sounds as if the state police bounced him."

I winced. Yes, Hogan liked being in charge in his own town. He kept a very friendly relationship with the Michigan State Police, but Joe could be right. In a case involving a crime that was sure to draw national attention, the state police might take over. Heck, the FBI could be taking over, and either agency could cut Hogan right out, even though the kidnapping occurred within his jurisdiction.

Besides, he'd been a witness to the kidnapping. The situation had to be humiliating for him.

So I waited for Hogan with some trepidation. But when he came in, he was his usual completely controlled self. He was definitely off duty, though. I could tell because he immediately ordered a small pepperoni pizza and a Labatt Blue to go with it. Hogan would never drink on duty.

Luckily, the younger generation was pretty much through eating, so Will, Carl, Tracy, and Brenda all left almost immediately.

Aunt Nettie, Hogan, Joe, and I gathered into a more compact group, and Hogan told us that the FBI had already been called in. "And I'm out," he said. "Completely. They won't even use my office as HQ."

"That's stupid of them," I said. "You know this town inside and out."

My sympathy didn't seem to be a lot of comfort. "I may know Warner Pier, but they know everything," Hogan said grimly.

"It's pretty obvious that the pirates took Marco off the yacht," Joe said.

I nodded. "That chest obviously must have been a piece of professional magic gear with a false bottom. All I can figure is that Marco met them on the swim platform and got into the chest voluntarily."

Joe nodded. "He could have ducked into the garage and waited for them. He probably figured he'd pop out of the chest at the end of the act. But the pirates didn't let him out."

"How could they keep him in it?"

"There was a hypodermic needle in the garage, so we assume they drugged him," Hogan said quietly. "Then we all stood around and applauded while they carried him off the yacht. And they cut the power to the radar so we couldn't keep track of which direction they went."

"How could they do that?"

"Somebody messed with the electrical panel. But that's not readily accessible to visitors on board."

"When did it go out?" Joe said.

"The captain's not sure. Everybody got distracted by the pirates' show."

"Could they have asked Marco to cut the power off himself?"

Hogan shrugged. "When Marco comes back, we'll ask him."

We were all silent for a moment. Then Joe spoke. "The next question is, where have they hidden him now?"

"That's why the feds think I'm just some stupid hick cop," Hogan said. "The pirates have been operating all summer. They've got to have a place to hide that inflatable dinghy and all their gear. But we've never figured out where."

"But, Hogan," Nettie said, "until tonight they weren't suspected of any crime. If you'd tried to track them down, you'd have been interfering with their constitutional rights."

"That doesn't cut much ice with the feds. Or with me, for that matter. I didn't need to arrest them, but I ought to know what's going on in my own town."

"It seems as if they'd need a fairly large place," Aunt Nettie said. "A boathouse would be best. Plus a place where three or four people could hide out for several days, since they'll need guards."

Joe chuckled, but it wasn't a humorous sound. "Sounds like my shop."

"No, Joe, your shop isn't remote enough," I said. "The neighbors could hear yelling from over there. Besides, you just have a dock, not a boathouse. I've always thought it was funny that boathouses are common back in Texas, where the weather is warm, and rare up here, where boats really need protection."

Joe nodded. "Our boats need so much protection in the winter that we hoist them out of the water. For other seasons, a tarp is enough cover."

I stared at the shaker of Parmesan cheese in the center of the table. We all sat glumly.

The theater group got up to leave, and Maggie and Ken stopped to talk. I tried to force myself to act normal. "Maggie! I hear you were directing tonight."

"Max came in toward the end."

"I did have a question. Mikki said Max didn't want *The Pirates of Penzance* to be campy. How can it not be? Isn't that the whole point of *Pirates*?"

I'll never know what Maggie answered, because as soon as the last sentence was out of my mouth I knew.

I knew where Marco was, and I knew who had kidnapped him.

Chapter 22

I thought Maggie and Ken were never going to leave. They kept standing there talking about comic opera, and I wanted to talk to Hogan about real life.

Hogan was eating pepperoni pizza, Aunt Nettie was drinking coffee, and Joe was finishing his beer. They were as worried as I was about Marco Spear, but each of them was managing to look placid in front of Maggie and Ken, who knew nothing about the kidnapping.

I don't know what I looked like, but internally I was a Texas tornado. My brain was whirling. I wanted to scream. Joe tells me I acted okay, although when Maggie told me that the character of the general in *The Pirates of Penzance* is supposedly based on an actual British military leader, I said, "Was the real guy a barleycorn? I mean, a baritone?" I guess Maggie left after that one. The comment certainly enhanced my reputation as the biggest ditz in Warner Pier.

As soon as Maggie and Ken were out the door, I leaned in toward the center of the table. I tried to whisper, but I may have hollered.

"Hogan! I know where they're hiding Marco!"

He didn't react as enthusiastically as I'd hoped. In fact, Hogan, Joe, and Aunt Nettie all looked as me as if I had completely lost my mind.

"I mean it!" I said. "I just realized it. I'm sure I know."

Hogan spoke calmly. "Okay, Lee. Tell us about it."

Suddenly I remembered why I had never told Hogan about my visit to Camp Sail-Along. It had included one of the most embarrassing moments in my entire life. But now I had to reveal all.

I sighed. "I didn't tell you about this, but last week I took a drive out to Camp Sail-Along."

"Exactly where is that?" Joe said.

"What is it?" Aunt Nettie said.

"Why?" Hogan said.

I answered Hogan's question. "Because of Jeremy's T-shirt," I said.

Quickly I explained that Jeremy had come into my office to bring Max a message, and he'd been wearing a Camp Sail-Along T-shirt.

"So after Joe and I became convinced that Jeremy had deliberately involved us in his fake drowning, I went out to the camp to ask if they knew anything about Jeremy, and I said something stupid."

I described my conversation with Jack McGrath, and how it had ended with an unusually awful slip of the tongue.

Aunt Nettie said, "Oh, dear, Lee!" Hogan drank some of his beer, obviously trying to hide a smile.

Joe laughed. "I shouldn't let you out alone," he said. "And I wouldn't, if I didn't know you're smart enough to get yourself out of these messes."

"In the Camp Sail-Along case, I jumped in the van and

drove off," I said. "But I didn't think I'd accomplished any-thing, except feeling sorry for Jack McGrath and humiliating myself, so I didn't mention the trip except to Joe. And I didn't tell him the embarrassing part."

"Why are you bringing it up now?"

"Partly because Camp Sail-Along—boathouse and lonely cabins . . . lonely cabins with padlocks on the doors—meets Aunt Nettie's description of the place needed to hold Marco prisoner until they get the ransom settled. And partly because I just placed the guy who looked familiar in that gymnastics team picture. The one that had Jeremy and Hal in it."

"Who else was in it?"

"Jack McGrath. The manager of Camp Sail-Along. He's older, of course, and he's grown a mustache."

"But, Lee, you looked at the cutline of that picture."

"No, Hogan, I didn't. You handed it to me, and I looked at Jeremy. I read his name—Matlock—and realized he was using Mattox as an alias. But before I read the rest of the names, Joe came in and told us he'd once represented Hal Weldon. I forgot all about the cutline. So I never realized the picture included Jack McGrath.

"Anyway, that picture connects Jeremy with Jack McGrath, and Jack McGrath runs that camp." I tapped my finger on the table for emphasis. "And I'm absolutely convinced Jeremy is mixed up in this deal."

Hogan looked at me evenly. "You haven't explained why."

I ticked off the reasons on my fingers. "First, Hal had a skull and crossbones tattoo, and he was a gymnast. He must have been the taller pirate. And Hal was the connection with Joe, since Joe had once represented him. Second, Hal and

Jeremy were friends; their landlady said they were working up an acrobatic act. Third, after Hal was shot, Jeremy arranged his own disappearance at the same spot where Hal's body had been dumped. You'll never get me to believe he didn't do that on purpose, to make sure his friend's body would be found."

Hogan nodded. "So you think that both Hal and Jeremy were mixed up with the pirates. There was some sort of falling out, and Hal was killed. Jeremy knew where his body had been dumped, and he arranged for it to be found."

"Right."

"You're trying to connect this to Camp Sail-Along, and to a major crime, with a T-shirt and an old teammate."

"There are a few more reasons. Hal's landlady—Ella Van Ark—said Hal moved out of the Riverside because he had a new job that included room and board. That would fit in with Camp Sail-Along."

"They should have plenty of spare bedrooms," Joe said. "And if they'd bought or leased the whole camp, they wouldn't have had to pay rent if another guy moved in."

"Yes. When Jack McGrath showed me around, he opened a door near the office in the main building, pointed inside, and said, 'My humble abode.' There was nothing much in the room but two cots. One of them was messy. Clothes scattered around, and bed unmade. The other was ultraneat. Blankets tucked military style, and a footlocker at the end of the bed. It definitely looked as if two very different people had been staying there."

Hogan frowned. "You think Jeremy and Hal planned the kidnapping?"

"No! In fact, I think they were trying to stop it."

"Go on," he said.

"Why else was Hal shot, for one thing? And why has Jeremy disappeared?" I dropped my voice again. "I think Jeremy must be dead. The mastermind of the kidnapping would be stupid not to kill him, too, once he'd tipped the cops—indirectly—to where Hal's body was. Unless Jeremy has managed to get away from 'the mastermind.'" I put finger quotes around the final words.

"No," Joe said. "Jeremy hasn't managed that, because he would have come out into the open. If Jeremy felt he was safe, he could have simply gone to a phone and called Hogan up to reveal the whole plan. Besides, Jeremy was one of the pirates who boarded the yacht tonight."

My head whipped toward Joe. "Are you sure?"

"Yes, I'm sure that the shorter pirate tonight was the same one who boarded our boat last June. He was the one who played the pennywhistle and danced. He did somersaults and other stunts. The 'mastermind,' as you call him, needs Jeremy. He needs his athletic skills. Maybe his musical skills, too."

"You're right!" I said. "Think of the pirates tonight. The one who came up from the swim platform first was no athlete. He did some dance moves, but he didn't stand on his hands or do a cartwheel or do anything that was precisely physical. In fact, he looked sort of tubby."

"Plus," Joe said, "the pirates didn't swim up and swim away tonight. They had to take the chest with them, true, but tonight's boarding followed a different pattern. No, Jeremy is still alive, and the pirates are using him—willingly or not."

"Which means he's in danger of being killed."

Hogan frowned. "Now, there's one part of all this that you haven't even mentioned, Lee. Why did someone lie in wait for you and Joe at Joe's dock?"

JoAnna Carl

"Hogan, I have no idea! I guess they did it because they were stupid! Certainly, at that point neither Joe nor I was any threat to anybody. And they sure made an amateurish try at hurting us."

Joe reached over and took my hand. "Hogan, the more I think about that episode, the more I think it wasn't meant to be that amateurish. I think they were expected to kill us."

"Joe!" I said. "That's ridiculous. The whole thing seemed like a joke."

"True. But I'll tell you, Lee, when that guy pointed a gun right at you from five or six feet away—and fired. Well, I nearly died of a heart attack."

"But it must have been a joke. You've said he couldn't have missed."

"No, he couldn't have. The only explanation is that the pistol wasn't loaded. The gun must have been loaded with blanks."

Hogan nodded. "Ever since you told that story, I've wondered if that wasn't true."

"And if Jeremy was involved," Joe said, "that becomes logical. Jeremy is a stagehand; he works with the technical side of theater. Finding, or even making, blank shells would be one of his skills."

Joe squeezed my hand, and I squeezed his back. Neither of us was going to get over that attack at the dock in a hurry.

Hogan leaned close. "Lee, what gave you a brainstorm? How did you figure all of this out—right this moment?"

"Mikki."

Everybody looked blank, and I went on.

"Mikki is afflicted with malapropism, Hogan, just like I am. Before you got here, she came over and talked to me. And twice she used the word 'campy.' Once her tongue slipped and she substituted 'campy' for 'catty,' and the other time she used it in its common meaning of overdone or phony."

"So?"

"We malapropists get used to making those slips of the tongue. We just go on, even if people laugh. When Mikki mixed up her words on earlier occasions, she just ignored it. But both times she used the word 'campy' tonight, she turned red, stammered around, and acted embarrassed."

"Then you think Mikki was the pirate queen?"

"No. She's too tall." I thought a moment. "Jill was the pirate queen. No, that won't work! When Hal's body was found, Jill swore she'd never seen him before. I believed her."

"That could have been true if Jill had never seen him except in his pirate disguise," Hogan said. "And that's possible, since he left the theater before she joined the company."

We all considered that. "I don't think she could have ignored his tattoo," I said doubtfully.

"But Jill didn't see the tattoo when we found Hal's body," Hogan said. "I didn't see it myself until after she'd left the beach."

"No! That still won't work." Joe shook his head vigorously. "Jill's too flat chested."

Aunt Nettie and I both laughed.

"Honestly!" she said. "Men never learn. As my mother used to say, 'What nature has forgotten, we just stuff with cotton.'"

"Sorry, Nettie," Joe said. "That wasn't cotton peeking out of the pirate queen's costume. It was genuine cleavage."

"Joe," I said, "did you ever hear of something called a push-up bra?"

"You mean her cleavage wasn't real?"

"Obviously her cleavage *was* real. But it could have been moved around. Pushed up."

"Pushed?"

"Yes, darling. That's why they call it a push-up bra. It shoves the boobs higher and to the center of the chest."

"Beauty queen contestants wear these things?"

"Sometimes. It depends on the rules of the contest. I never wore one! But you can buy them at Penney's. Anyway, Jill could have been the pirate queen, and Jeremy must have been the pirate who played the pipe, danced, and did somersaults. Hal was originally the larger pirate, the big guy who did the most athletic stunts. The one who yelled, 'Yo-ho-ho!' Either Jill hadn't seen him without his costume and makeup, or she pretended not to know who he was when she was shown his body."

Hogan spoke. "Since we're assigning roles, and Hal's dead, do you have a name for the guy who took over as the lead pirate tonight?"

I surprised myself with the name that popped out. "Jack McGrath. He's got to be involved, since he's the one staying at the camp. He has the right build, if he added some padding. Again, we're talking theatrical people. They'd know how to add padding."

Silence fell again. I stared at Hogan. Had I convinced him? Could he do anything about it? Or would he see some fatal flaw in my reasoning and throw out my whole elaborate plot?

Joe, Aunt Nettie, and I all sat silently. Hogan was thinking so hard, I could practically hear his brain whirring. When he finally cleared his throat and leaned over, we all jumped.

"You know, Lee, this is all pretty vague. I don't think it's proof enough to justify raiding that camp tonight."

"Do you think you could get a search warrant for the camp?"

"At this moment, I couldn't get a search warrant to look at that yacht, and it's a crime scene."

Joe took a deep breath, as if he was going to say something, but he didn't. There was no reason for him to point out in his lawyerly way that law officers don't need warrants to search crime scenes. Hogan knew that as well as Joe did.

We all sat a few minutes. Then Hogan abruptly downed the last of his Labatt's. "Let's go over to the office," he said. "Maybe I can talk to the state cops."

So we paid our bill and left. For the next half hour, Joe, Aunt Nettie, and I sat in Hogan's outer office. Hogan closed himself inside his inner office. We could see that the phone was lit up, and once or twice we heard the rumble of his voice. But Hogan didn't come out and tell us that the FBI and the Michigan State Police were ready to raid Camp Sail-Along.

When he did come out, he didn't look happy. "The best I could get was a promise to look at it tomorrow," he said.

He threw himself down in a chair, and the four of us stared at one another some more.

Then Hogan spoke. "Joe, do you know the river channel up to Lake o' the Winds?"

"Yep. I take all the boats I work on up to that lake for a test run."

"You willing to try it tonight?"

"Sure."

"Maybe we could take a little scouting trip up that way,"

Hogan said. He held up a warning finger. "Now, we're definitely not getting too close to the camp."

"Of course not," Joe said. "We'll keep our distance. But we can take the night-vision glasses, can't we?"

Hogan nodded grimly. "Sure. They're on loan from the state police. It seems very suitable to take them along."

Chapter 23

I'm not at all sure why Aunt Nettie and I were allowed to go on the excursion to Camp Sail-Along. In fact, I'm not sure why Joe was allowed to go, except that he owned the boat and knew the river channel. Maybe Hogan wanted to be able to tell the Michigan State Police and the feds that he'd just made a casual trip that evening, even took the wives along.

None of us was dressed warmly enough to be out on the water in a semi-open boat at eleven o'clock at night. By then the temperature was in the mid-fifties. Hogan rounded up some extra cop jackets, the kind with POLICE in big letters on the fronts and backs, and off we went, headed for Joe's boat shop and the Shepherd Sedan tied up at its dock.

The first part of the trip, of course, was the tricky bit as far as boating goes, since Joe had to take us about a mile up the river before we reached the channel into Lake o' the Winds. That stretch of the Warner River is broader than it is deep, and the banks are lined with all sorts of plants that can enmesh a boat or tear up its propeller.

At least the night was clear. The moon was in the west-ern half of the sky and was casting lovely reflections on the water. Joe kept the sedan's motor at a steady gurgle—slow and cautious—and he swept the banks with his spotlight. It wouldn't have been a bad ride, if we hadn't been afraid of what we'd find when we got to Camp Sail-Along. Or afraid that we wouldn't find anything.

When we got within sight of the lake, Joe throttled the motor back to a murmur and motioned that he wanted to speak to Hogan and me.

"This place is on the south side of the lake, right?"

Hogan and I nodded.

"I don't remember anyplace over there with a big boathouse. In fact, there's not a lot over there at all."

"Yes, it's lonely," I said. "That's what makes it ideal for this crime."

"I'm not sure about the boathouse," Hogan said. "I've never had any reason to go there, either from the lake or from the land side. I just know where the road turns in from McIntosh Road. Lee? You've made the most recent visit."

I closed my eyes and tried to remember. "There's a big storage shed down near the water, Joe. I saw it from the land side, of course, and there may be trees between that big shed and the lake. But there's a smaller building that definitely is a boathouse."

"Is it big enough to hold the pirates' inflatable?"

"Oh, yes. Maybe the best landmark from the water would be that long dock that could be used to tie up six or eight small sailboats—back when it was a camp."

"Oh, yeah! The long dock. I know the place."

The sedan's motor began to gurgle again, and we entered the lake. With a smooth expanse of water about a half mile in diameter, there was plenty of room for the moon to make a gorgeous pathway across the lake. Many of the houses on the north edge of the lake had outdoor lights, of course, and some of their windows still were lit. All the lights were doubled; we could see the lights plus their reflections. The northern half of the lake sparkled.

The scene was beautiful but scary. I thought of those quiet homes with normal families—watching television, reading books, sleeping—while a half mile across the lake a nest of killers and kidnappers was lurking.

I tried to remind myself that I might be wrong. There might be nothing wrong going on at Camp Sail-Along. My teeth began to chatter anyway.

Hogan spoke. "Go around to the north, Joe. Let's not go directly to the camp."

Joe nodded, and the sedan swung toward the left. Hogan took out the nightscope. He moved to the small deck at the stern and knelt. He mounted the scope on its tripod and pointed it toward the camp.

I whispered to Joe, "Do you want to take a turn on the scope?"

He nodded, then got up, and I slid under the sedan's steering gear. The boat is easy to operate. The whole point of the sedan is that it's like driving a car.

I kept the boat moving slowly along the north shore, where the houses were. Joe and Hogan knelt on the deck and took turns looking the camp over with the scope. Aunt Nettie sat still. I think all of us were holding our breaths.

I came to the east end of the lake and followed the shore, turning south. Now I could see the site of Camp Sail-Along without craning my neck. Or I would have been able to see the site if it hadn't been dark. In the moonlight I could barely make out the boathouse, with its metal roof reflecting the moonlight, and the long, narrow dock.

The sedan gurgled its way to within a hundred yards or so of the south shore, and I turned west. Now the camp was straight ahead of me and a little to the left. Everything was quiet. I began to think I'd ask for a turn with the night-vision scope.

Then I heard two things.

First, the *kerthump-kerthump* of running feet.

Second, a splash.

"What was that?" I used a stage whisper.

Joe hissed out an answer. "Somebody ran down that dock and jumped off!"

There were more running feet.

And the sound of a shot echoed over the water.

"Lee, speed up," Hogan's voice was urgent but not loud. "Cut the lights and head for the camp!"

My hand shook as I turned off the lights—all the lights, even the ones required by the rules of boat safety. I pulled the throttle out slightly, but I was afraid to gun the motor.

Then Hogan popped up beside me. "Watch my directions," he said. "There's a guy in the water, and we'll have to try to pick him up."

"Joe!" My voice squeaked. "You'll have to take over!"

"You can handle it." His voice sounded a lot more confident than I felt.

I increased the boat's speed again, and I looked back to see Joe drop his pants.

Oh, no! Joe was getting ready to go into the water to pull the man out. I didn't like that idea.

More running and some yelling was happening on the

shore. And a few minutes earlier someone had fired a gun, apparently at the man in the water. I didn't want Joe to become a second target.

Hogan pushed the sedan's windshield open and poked his head out. He made a chopping motion with his hand, signaling for me to turn farther to the right.

Then he leaned down, close to my ear, so that I could hear him over the motor. "Not too fast," he said. "The guy's afloat. We don't want to run him down."

Looking ahead, I could see nothing but the moon on the water. Then a dark lump broke its silvery path. The water around the lump was disturbed.

The man in the water was thrashing around.

I pointed the boat directly toward him. "Steady," Hogan said. "Steady. Not too fast. You're doing fine."

Then another shot was fired. I gave a wordless yelp. And I increased the throttle speed just slightly.

I felt Hogan and Joe's urgency. We had to get that guy out of the water, and we had to do it right that minute.

"A little to the left!" Hogan's voice commanded me. "Circle around him. Put the boat between him and the shore. Nettie! You get that life jacket on! And get down!"

It did cross my mind to wonder what good a life jacket would do if we went into that cold, spring-fed lake. I expected to die of the shock.

I also wondered whether Aunt Nettie could swim. I'd never known her to go to the beach—even to wade.

And I wondered whether bullets would bounce off life jackets.

But I obeyed Hogan's directions and managed to get the boat between the man in the water and the shore. Then I cut the throttle to idle, and we lingered where we were, floating at the mercy of whatever currents moved through the lake.

Just as I swung into place, I heard a splash. When I looked back, Joe was no longer kneeling at the gunwale. He'd gone into the water.

It had been fifteen years since Joe had worked as a lifeguard. I breathed a prayer, asking that he hadn't forgotten his skills. An injured man wasn't going to be easy to get out of the water.

Hogan rushed down the center aisle. The boat tipped and bucked. I couldn't see what was happening.

I heard a cry. It wasn't very loud, but it sounded like agonizing pain. Then there were words, words spoken by a new voice. "Oh, God!"

"Sorry, guy," Hogan said. "We're going to get you out of here!"

I looked back. I could see dark legs lying flat on the deck. Joe and Hogan had been able to lift the man into the boat. He was alive. And he was in pain. I was relieved, but I knew the crisis wasn't over.

Then the boat bucked and tipped again. I saw Joe flop over the stern onto the deck.

At that same moment, another shot was fired, and a bullet hit our bow.

"Lee!" Joe shouted. "Dig out!"

I dug.

I didn't worry about lights. I just looked at the moon and tried to guess what direction was west.

I was mighty grateful when Joe came to the front of the boat. I knew I could never run that weedy, crooked river channel in the dark. Heck, I doubted I could do it in broad daylight.

Since Joe was at the helm, I moved back to the deck. This

wasn't the easiest thing to do, with the sedan traveling at top speed, but I felt that someone should pay attention to the wounded man.

Aunt Nettie beat me to him. He had rolled onto his side and curled into a ball. He was bleeding from a wound in his back.

Joe's shirt was lying on the deck. It wasn't exactly sterile, but this didn't seem to be the moment to worry about that. I folded the shirt into a thick pad and used it to apply pressure to the wound. Aunt Nettie had pulled off her police jacket, and she draped it over the man's shoulders like a blanket.

I saw that he was wearing jeans. I remember thinking that the guy must be a champion swimmer; if I went into the drink in jeans, I'd sink straight to the bottom. We needed to get those heavy denim pants off him—they must be like wearing sheets of ice—but this didn't seem to be the moment for that either.

Suddenly a bright light washed over us.

We'd been hit by a spotlight. "Get down!" Hogan must have shouted, because we heard him. And I could hear the roar of a boat's motor, and it wasn't the gurgle-gurgle of the sedan.

Aunt Nettie dropped to her stomach, but ol' dumb Lee looked up to see what was happening.

And what was happening was that the inflatable—the pirate ship—was racing toward us. It must have come out of the boathouse, and it was heading toward us fast. Of course, I couldn't see it clearly, because I was blinded by its spotlight. I only knew what must be happening.

The inflatable's modern, high-powered outboard motor was maybe twice as fast as the sedan's antique gurgling inboard.

They could run us down in about two minutes.

And they had guns.

I've had moments when I thought my life was absolutely at an end. The night my high school friend almost hit the bridge abutment. The night my pal Lindy and I went over an embankment, skidded through the bushes, and came to rest on the January ice of Lake Michigan. The time the snowmobile chased me. The time when—well, there have been times I'd rather not remember.

But the fifteen seconds after I saw that inflatable headed after us—I'd rather not remember those moments, but I can't forget them.

Then Hogan yelled again. "Get down!" I ducked, but I looked at him at the same time, and I realized something important.

We had guns, too.

Hogan was a lawman. He routinely carried a gun.

Hogan pulled out his pistol. He knelt and aimed at the inflatable. Then he fired. Nothing happened. Then he fired again. And their spotlight went out.

One moment I was completely blind because of the glare of the spotlight. The next I couldn't see a thing because the bright light had gone out.

The noise of the boats was terrific. The sedan was still racing across the lake, its motor as loud as it ever gets, and the inflatable was coming after us, its outboard twice as loud as ours.

Hogan was still kneeling in the stern. He took another shot. For a moment nothing happened. Then Hogan fired again.

And the inflatable began to go nuts. It swung around crazily.

Hogan fired off another shot.

Suddenly the inflatable was farther from us. A shot rang out from its direction, but it didn't seem to come anyplace near us.

I could see two men on board. They moved to the left side of the craft, then to the right.

Finally, one of them seemed to remember the motor. He turned it off, and the whole chase grew a lot more silent. Then one of the guys dived overboard, over on the side farthest from us. The second man kept moving back and forth. I had the feeling that he was wringing his hands, trying to decide what to do.

Meanwhile, the inflatable was losing air rapidly. The right side was growing as limp as a sail on a becalmed boat.

Then the whole thing flipped over.

Hogan yelled at Joe, telling him to stop, but Joe had apparently seen what was going on, and he'd already cut the sedan's motor to idle. He walked back to the deck and stood beside Hogan.

He looked pretty ridiculous, wearing nothing but a pair of boxer briefs, soaking wet and quite revealing, and a jacket that said POLICE on the back.

"I'm tempted to let them drown," he said, "but I guess we'd better try to pull 'em out."

Chapter 24

Police chiefs are handy guys to have around in emergencies. Not only did Hogan have a gun; he had a radio. Plus, he'd already stationed Patrolman Jerry Cherry of the Warner Pier PD on McIntosh Road, outside the entrance to Camp Sail-Along. Jerry heard the shots, then got a radio call from Hogan, so he had driven into the camp and was waiting at the long dock when we got there. The Warner County Sheriff's Department, the Michigan State Police, and the Warner Pier Paramedics were on the way.

We pulled one man from the lake. As I'd suspected, it was Jack McGrath. He didn't appear to be hurt by his dunking, but he was noticeably glad to be picked up. It seemed he wasn't much of a swimmer.

The other man—the one who'd jumped out of the inflatable dinghy early—had disappeared. I feared that they'd be dragging the lake for him. We ran the spotlight over the water, but we saw no sign of him. Jack wouldn't say who he was.

Hogan produced handcuffs—his stock of equipment never seemed to end—and attached Jack McGrath to the sedan's anchor. Then he held a gun on him while Aunt Nettie and I continued to do what we could in the line of first aid for the man who had been shot, and Joe guided the sedan to the Camp Sail-Along dock, which was the closest place where an ambulance could meet us. Lights were flashing on at the houses across the lake, but as yet no one who lived over there had come roaring across in a boat. Something about all the shots that had been fired had probably discouraged the peaceful Lake o' the Winds community from coming to find out the reason for all the roaring boat motors. Hogan said the county 9-1-1 operator was getting lots of calls.

The wounded man, as I'd been assuming, said he was the long-lost Jeremy. I felt quite relieved to learn that he was still alive.

The Camp Sail-Along dock sat in a forest of waterweeds, but Joe sidled up to it. As soon as he tied up, Hogan and Jerry marched Jack McGrath ashore and locked him in Jerry's patrol car.

Joe aimed the sedan's spotlight toward Aunt Nettie and me and our patient, away from the shore, so that we had some light. He picked up his good khaki slacks, which had been kicked into the corner of the deck, stepped out onto the dock, and walked away into the darkness. I assumed he planned to take his wet undershorts off and put the khakis on without shocking Aunt Nettie. Actually, he could have done this on the boat and she wouldn't have turned a hair, but men can be modest at the oddest times.

Aunt Nettie and I continued to kneel beside the wounded Jeremy. We could already hear sirens in the distance.

I leaned close to Jeremy. "The ambulance will be here in a minute," I said.

He gave a painful sigh. "Thanks. As long as that bastard doesn't get away."

"Jack McGrath? He's locked in the patrol car."

"Jack? He doesn't matter. It's the old bastard I want. The one who got me into this."

Jeremy seemed to drift off into semiconsciousness at that point, leaving me to figure out what he'd been talking about. "The old bastard?" Who could he mean?

When Hogan, Joe, and I had been figuring out whodunit, we'd assigned roles to Jeremy, to Hal, and to Jill. I still felt sure that they were the three pirates who'd boarded the sedan back on Midsummer's Eve. Then we had decided that Jack McGrath was the other person involved in the boardings. He hadn't been a pirate, but he'd been needed to run the hideout at Camp Sail-Along, and he'd helped lift the magic chest holding Marco Spear off the yacht.

Now I counted noses and realized that there had been a fifth person in the kidnapping gang.

This was the person who had been in the inflatable with Jack McGrath when Hogan shot it out of the water.

We'd all seen the second person go overboard. But who was he?

Could it have been Jill?

I closed my eyes and pictured the inflatable as the air poured out of one side of it. No, I felt sure that the person who had dived overboard had been a man.

So, who had it been?

I checked Joe's shirt, the pad I was holding against Jeremy's back. All I knew to do was apply pressure, and that improvised pad was getting completely soaked.

I muttered. "Where's that ambulance?"

Jeremy opened his eyes. "He promised big," he said. "He had the contacts. But it was just a plot to get Hal and me into it. We even found Jack for him. Then he killed Hal."

His eyes closed; then they opened. "Do you have any water?"

"I'm afraid you shouldn't have any, Jeremy. They'll be giving you an IV pretty quick."

"I really am thirsty. A whole pitcher of that sangria sure would be good." He seemed to drift off.

Pitcher. Someone else had mentioned drinks that came in a pitcher. Someone who hadn't been on the yacht and therefore hadn't had a chance to drink any.

Max. In the Dock Street Pizza Place he'd mentioned hors d'oeuvres and pitchers of drinks.

Was that a coincidence?

My heart began to pound.

Max Morgan had to be the other pirate. I was sure of it. It hadn't been Jack who replaced Hal as the lead pirate, the one who did stunts and yelled out "Yo-ho-ho!" Jack couldn't have handled the dramatic gestures the pirate made on board the yacht that night.

The new leader of the pirates had been Max Morgan, disguised with a lot of fake beard, hair, and eyebrows, plus a fat belly. A fat belly like the one Max had worn when he played Falstaff.

"The old bastard." That described him accurately. Plus, Max was a longtime theater pro. To young people like Jeremy or Jill, he would appear to have "contacts."

Had Max set up this whole plot? Had he organized the pirates, used them over the whole summer to entertain and lull Warner Pier's boating community into complacency? Because now it was obvious that the whole pirate stunt, the boardings that had amused us all summer, were a plan to kidnap Marco Spear.

"Max." I murmured the word.

Immediately the sedan began to bounce again, and water began to splash over the swim platform. My head twisted toward the sound so quickly that my neck nearly unscrewed.

"Max!" This time I screamed the word.

Max Morgan had climbed over the swim platform and was in the boat with Jeremy, Aunt Nettie, and me.

And he still had his pistol.

"Okay!" His voice wasn't loud, but its tone was as cold as that spring-fed lake water. "Forget that creep there on the floor, and get this boat under way."

"No!" I yelled it. Maybe someone—Joe, Hogan, Jerry— would hear me. "Max, I can't operate this boat."

"You were running it earlier."

"I can't get it out of the lake! The channel is too tricky! I'll run aground."

"I know the channel! You start the motor!"

"No! I can't!"

Max pointed his pistol at Aunt Nettie's head. He didn't say anything. He didn't need to.

I got to my feet, moving as slowly as I could.

Max spoke again. "Move!"

I backed down the aisle, toward the controls. "You'll have to untie the mooring line."

"Your sweet little aunt can do it!" He poked her with the pistol.

Aunt Nettie got up and went to the side of the boat. Obediently, she began to unwind the mooring line from its stanchion. I felt for the key, hoping that Joe had taken it out and put it in his pocket. But no, it was in the ignition, waiting. I realized that had been a vain hope. After all, Joe hadn't had his pants on when he turned the motor off. But maybe . . . I pulled the key out, juggled it around and dropped it on the floor of the boat. "I've dropped the key!"

"Bitch! Find it! And use it!"

I fumbled on the floor. There was no way to claim I couldn't find the key; it was attached to a key chain with a large fish-shaped charm on it, the kind that floats. All boat keys should have one of those, so the key won't sink if you drop it overboard.

Max moved closer to me, still spewing swearwords. At that moment the sedan began to buck again. I'd learned what that meant—someone was climbing in.

Max knew what it meant, too. He whirled toward the back of the boat.

No one was there. Aunt Nettie was standing on the deck with one hand behind her back, looking as innocent as a sweet little old lady can.

"Get that motor going!" Max turned back toward me.

As he rotated around, Aunt Nettie pulled that wonderful short oar from behind her, swung it like a baseball bat, and aimed for the fences. She hit Max right between the shoulder blades with the edge of the oar.

The next moments were really confusing. Max fell forward, landing with his chin on the back of one of the sedan's seats and popping his neck back. Then he rolled over onto his side. The trigger of his pistol clicked, but it didn't go off.

I jumped on top of him, straddled his chest, and put one of my knees on each of his arms. He'd have to throw me off before he could go anywhere.

Joe, naked and covered with waterweeds, came over the side of the boat. He tried to grab Max, but Max was lying in the aisle with me on top of him. All Joe could touch were Max's feet. He began to tug at him, trying to slide Max toward the deck. Since he had to pull me along as well—all my weight was on Max—this proved to be a pretty hard job.

Aunt Nettie yelled for help.

Hogan and Jerry ran down the dock. Sirens grew louder until they became deafening. I saw lights—whirling blue lights and brilliant white headlights. They looked beautiful. They meant more law enforcement was there.

They looked even more beautiful when Hogan and Jerry Cherry found Marco Spear, still drugged and sleeping peacefully, in one of the derelict camp cabins. It had been fixed up quite comfortably, they said. Obviously the kidnappers were ready to hold Marco for a week or more.

Aunt Nettie, of course, was the heroine of the whole thing, and her picture ran on the front pages of—apparently—every newspaper in the United States. She and Hogan gave a press conference the next day, hoping to calm things down. She posed holding the oar. But it was useless. Finally, she and Hogan took off before dawn in a borrowed car and went to Arizona, where they hid out at the home of Hogan's niece.

After they disappeared, the press turned their attention to Joe and me. We borrowed his mom's car, left Aunt Nettie's chief assistant in charge of TenHuis Chocolade, and went down to Texas to see my dad in Prairie Creek. Prairie Creek people are closemouthed with strangers. And strangers stand out because there are so few of them.

In a week things had calmed down, and we were all able to come home.

Jeremy was the other hero. He was in a Holland hospital for quite a while, but doctors promised he would recover fully. Marco was kept overnight in the same hospital, and I'm happy to say that before he left the next morning, Marco not only went to visit Jeremy, but promised to help him get a job in Hollywood. One photographer was allowed in, so they had their picture taken together. The caption was "High school teammate saves kidnapped movie star."

Plus, the studio came up with a reward for Jeremy. So Jeremy came out okay, though he required four pints of blood that first night. The bullet had hit an important artery, but no vital organs.

As his mutterings in the boat had revealed, Jeremy had been enticed into the pirate business by Max, who told him it was all to be a joke. When Jeremy and Hal realized a real crime was planned, Hal was afraid to go to the police, partly because of his earlier involvement in the big Viking prank in Chicago. Hal tried to contact Joe, but Max found out what he was up to. Max shot him, then forced Jeremy to help dump his friend's body. Jeremy managed to dump him near Beech Tree Public Access Area so his body could be found. When Jeremy tried to fake his own death so he could get away from the plot, Max figured out where he was hiding and forced him to continue. Jeremy had been kept at Camp Sail-Along, with Jack McGrath in charge. Jeremy had pretended to be cooperating, but on the one occasion he slipped away from Jack in Warner Pier—late at night—he wrote that odd warning note and stuck it in the door of TenHuis Chocolade. Because Hal knew Joe, Jeremy had felt that Joe could be trusted to help him. Both Hal and Jeremy had been afraid of facing criminal charges because of their involvement with Max's plot.

The loan shark—never seen by anyone but Max—was invented to make Jeremy's disappearance credible. Joe and I are still convinced that Max simply described George Raft. He had a thing for old movies.

Jeremy insisted that Jill hadn't realized what was going on.

He had told her to go to Joe and me for help after he staged his drowning, Jeremy admitted, but to get her to do it, he was forced to say that Max wanted it done. Again, Jill had been promised a chance at Hollywood if she took part in the pirate boardings. She'd been told that taking Marco off in the magic chest was part of a publicity stunt. And Jill claimed she had never seen Hal when he wasn't in his pirate costume. He'd always been suited up when she and Jeremy appeared for their pirate excursions. I wasn't sure I believed that. Jill had to answer a lot of questions, but she was never charged.

Miraculously, the final Showboat production of *The Pirates of Penzance* came off. At the request of the Showboat owners, Maggie McNutt took over as director-producer, plus playing the part of Ruth. They opened on schedule, even with a completely demoralized cast. Maggie says the Showboat owners will have to find a new director for next year, and she hopes they come up with an honest one.

Mikki apparently was largely in the dark about the whole kidnapping scheme, but she had deduced that Jill was involved in some hanky-panky that involved a camp. This led to her embarrassment when she made a malaprop reference using the word "campy."

Jack McGrath made a plea bargain and got ten years. Daren Roberts also copped a plea. He had given Max inside information about Marco's schedule—including the original tip that Marco was coming to Warner Pier. Daren tried to say he'd done it innocently, but he had carelessly left a fingerprint on the door to the cabinet that concealed the electrical controls aboard Marco's yacht. This was pretty firm proof that he was the person who sabotaged the radar.

Max is still waging a legal battle, but Joe says he expects Max to receive a life sentence for kidnapping and murder.

"I wouldn't want to defend him," he said. "It would be tough."

Would Max have allowed Jeremy, Jill, or Jack to live after he no longer needed them to act as pirates?

I doubt it. They knew too much. Jeremy was convinced that Max was ready to kill him as soon as the kidnapping was accomplished. Because of that, he made a break for it. That's when Max shot him. Fate—or dumb luck—decreed that Joe, Hogan, Aunt Nettie, and I were close enough to rescue him before he grew too weak to swim.

A month after all the excitement, one more important event took place at Warner Pier. Marco came back to town, without the buckteeth and with his contact lenses. The trip wasn't given any publicity, but he invited all of us to dinner in Herrera's private dining room. The next day a ceremonial bottle of Michigan wine was broken on the bow of the new yacht—by Aunt Nettie—and a word was added to the yacht's name, at least temporarily.

Now it's *The Chocolate Buccaneer*.

Marco boarded then, and the yacht headed out on its maiden voyage, through the Great Lakes and the St. Lawrence Seaway to the Atlantic. It was to go on through the Panama Canal and wind up in the Port of Los Angeles. Of course, Marco didn't get to make the whole trip. He had to fly back to Hollywood to earn enough money to support his yacht.

And Marco has other major expenses. TenHuis Chocolade now has a standing order for a pound of chocolates to be delivered to the yacht—at any port in the world—once a month.

Chocolate Chat
Michigan's Foods Distinctive

Michigan's status in manufacturing is well-known, but it's also an important farming state, and the inhabitants, such as Joe and Lee, and the visitors, such as JoAnna Carl, take full advantage of this.

Michigan is a major fruit-growing region, and fruit pies, jams, and jellies, plus—oh, glory!—fresh fruit are apt to be on any menu. The state produces apples, pears, cherries, apricots, grapes, blackberries, blueberries, strawberries, raspberries, plums, and, my favorite, peaches. And I'm sure I'm leaving some important ones out. From Memorial Day until Columbus Day, something local and delicious is available.

Many fruits may be served dipped in chocolate, but they need no embellishment.

Ask a Michigan native to name the state's favorite food, however, and the answer is likely to be "brats." Bratwurst is frequently served, and it's delicious, particularly grilled over charcoal and tucked into a bun, with or without grilled onions.

But to me the most unusual Michigan dish is the olive burger. The bun is liberally smeared with mayonnaise, and the hamburger patty is topped with melted cheese, then with sliced green olives, the kind stuffed with pimiento. It's yummy!